CHAPTERS

Every relationship has untold secrets

ISBN: 978-1-7776276-0-7

eBook: 978-1-7776276-1-4

Dedicated to the Dreams, Desires, and Beliefs!

TABLE OF CONTENTS

Author's Note

If anything is complicated in this world, it is relationships. Okay, not all relationships are complicated, but many are. They also form the most important part of our lives, starting right from childhood to old age. This book presents the various angles of a love relationship, covering different phases, cycles, and ages. It is fascinating how different relationships, especially romantic ones, leave a permanent mark in our memory.

This is my first book as an author, a dream I saw in grade 11 or maybe 12. I told my teacher I wanted to write a book without knowing any details about the writing process and completely unaware of the topic I wanted to write about. My dream stayed with me throughout the growing-up days. As I got into blogs and article writing, I wondered when I could write a book.

Small notes saved in my Gmail and on my laptop became the chapters that are presented in this book. I enjoy scribbling my thoughts and never knew I could convert them into a book. While some relationship stories are fictional, most of them are true, inspired by real-life incidents.

It has taken a while to publish this book, but it has given me immense joy and a feeling of pride. With this book, I want to address the people who believe in love. I hope they can find their most special part of life in one or more chapters of this book, and relive them, or understand the other side of the story. Sometimes, it is good to know that others had a similar story, too.

I am thankful to all those who have contributed and have been part of this journey, whether it was listening to me while I shared my struggle with them, contributing their part of the story, or helping me with tips and suggestions.

I hope you will enjoy reading this book as much as I have enjoyed writing it!

"I believe that everything happens for a reason. People change so that you can learn to let go, things go wrong so that you appreciate them when they're right, you believe lies so you eventually learn to trust no one but yourself, and sometimes good things fall apart so better things can fall together."

— Marilyn Monroe

INTRODUCTION

*"The most important things are
the hardest to say!"* —Stephen King

We all have loved in our lives and have had amazing love stories, beautiful dreams, hurts, and betrayals. There are feelings we like to talk about and share with everyone, but some inner thoughts, desires, hurts, and emotions remain buried in our hearts.

We seldom talk about them for the fear of getting judged or misunderstood. Some feelings are hard to describe because it takes maturity and an open mind to understand the emotions during a particular situation; some unspoken hurts and heartfelt desires are usually inexplicable.

In our lives, love touches us in different ways. It touches us in the form of the friendship of a special friend or as a stranger we meet every day at the bus stop; love affects us by giving us pain that a lover's absence brings; it is also in the fear of losing someone.

To define love is difficult. So many emotions bundled up

together in the form of infatuation, serious love, hurt, betrayal, cheating, etc. emerge in different situations for different people. When the right string hits the right chord, you experience powerful emotions for your soulmate. And when love hits you, it leaves you spellbound.

Love will happen soon to you if you still haven't experienced this emotion and are waiting for it to touch your life. Everyone experiences the love syndrome at least once in their lifetime, some even twice or three times. However, first love is special and precious for most of us. Some people remain confused and do not realize they are in love until their special someone leaves them or shows interest in someone else while still being with them.

This happens with close friends who refuse to go beyond friendship and remain in that friend zone. When they realize this emotion, the journey from friends to lovers often looks complicated, especially if it is one-sided love.

We often dream about spending life with someone from our past; we may imagine a relationship with an ex-lover we left behind a long time ago. Some hurts and betrayals still make us cry; a few cheating episodes still make us wary of getting into a serious relationship. While some marriages are made in heaven, some make us wonder what we were thinking when we married our partners!

Every person has hidden feelings and chapters that they do not talk about. This book is my honest attempt to express and bring out the unspoken feelings and emotions in the form of chapters from individuals who opened up on the condition of anonymity. I am thankful to all those who opened their hearts to talk about the little stops in their journey, expressed their deep feelings, shed tears while narrating their parts, and those who trusted me with their deep secrets. Few stories are of my close friends with whom I share a special bond; some stories are a mix of real-life incidents and fiction, but most of them are one hundred percent true.

If you know me, you will identify which story is yours. Even if I am just an author to you, a random chapter may appeal to you as your own story! You most likely can relate to every emotion expressed and understand and feel the happiness, pain, and sadness of each character in each chapter if love has touched you even once. I hope you find your story in this book. Happy reading!

LOVE

In love we win, in love we lose;
In love we rise, in love we fall...!

1

The Unconfessed Love Story

It is your birthday today! A special date I never forget, no matter how much I try; a day I never missed because it was special not just for you, but for me, too. However, with the big shift in time, situation, and attitude, I think of forgetting your birthday every year and moving on.

Every year, I tell myself to ignore the date and consider your birthday as a normal day. I decide every time to not wish you a happy birthday, but I end up sending you a text message along with a *'how are you?'* message, starting a conversation you don't wish to have. Why do I start a series of texts when you are no longer interested in talking to me?

No matter how hard I try to chat in minimum words, the

conversation gets too long. I shouldn't do that, especially because you show no interest in asking about me. I still remember your long-distance calls to me that would last an hour, sometimes two, taking much of my time, but I made sure I listened to you and also talked about my days.

All this when there existed nothing between us. We were not in a committed or an extra-marital relationship, yet you would refuse to hang up when I sounded busy. You were so concerned about me when your commitment should have been toward your wife who you recently married. You knew about my commitments, too, but you defied everything to stay in touch with me.

What stops you from speaking to me now? You never confessed your love to me, yet you were talking to me on the day of your wedding. You made more calls to me than to your spouse when you were lonely, living by yourself in England. Whatever was between us was unsaid. There was no name for our relationship. We married our respective lovers, but we could not stop loving each other and kept the channel of communication smooth and open between us.

What suddenly changed between you and me? Who grew distant in our 'no name' relationship? Was it you or was it me? I do not wish to turn back the clock to a younger age, but my heart aches to figure out what changed you and your emotions. How did we become what we are today? The memories we created together continue to occupy a special place in our hearts.

They have passed the test of time and continue to delight us today. Isn't it amazing to have an unconfessed love story that we both acknowledged in our own way! We both realized how it felt to be around each other, but I guess words invariably fell short to express the true emotions. I wonder why it was so difficult to talk about our feelings.

How I wish we could once again enjoy the same childhood, where it all began—our innocent love story! Childhood—a phase where no one suspects you of secretly loving someone and dreaming about marrying them. From young lovers to mature adults, we walked through all phases of life, but never poured our hearts out.

How about we meet and pour our hearts out about the feelings that remain buried inside, talk about why and how the equation between us changed, and share why, despite the deep love, there was never a confession or a relationship!

This unconfessed love story continues to be close to my heart. We are growing old, and the only aspiration in my heart is to talk about our incomplete love story and open up about why you no longer talk to me!

"Some love stories are best left incomplete..."

2

The Unspoken Words

Have you ever wondered about the love behind the unspoken words? Do you think love needs any language? No matter how old and clichéd it sounds, it is true. Love has no language.

When a baby is born, they don't understand what their mother speaks, yet they can feel her love, touch, and heartbeats. Friends can sense each other's anxiety and mood swings. A dog can sense its master's love and its master's mood, too. Love is magical; it touches us in different ways and reshapes our lives, dreams, and behaviors.

Love is not about talking or expressing through words, but rather it is about emotions. We all have been through phases when a simple smile or even eye contact did the trick and lovers seldom-used words. Isn't it amazing that words do not define the connection between hearts; we sense when someone is in love with us just by looking at them or observing their expressions.

There was love in those missed landline calls, there was love when he watched me silently from the edge of the room. It was love when he lost the game for me and looked into my eyes to congratulate me; it was love when I would desperately wait for his one glance. Love made me look into his eyes and he reciprocated by maintaining eye contact; there was love when he unwittingly held my hand and refused to leave. Love, love, and just love, but no words.

We never expressed our feelings through words and we never formally got into a relationship. All we did was communicate through our eyes and with indirect talks that hinted toward our mutual fondness for each other. We realized the intimate relationship between our hearts but never talked about it or expressed it. Maybe we never considered confessing an important part of loving someone.

That could be the reason our relationship never hit the

road. We stayed in touch and checked on each other despite living miles apart, but there were no strings attached. When emotions ran high, we would talk over the phone but never acknowledge the truth—we were in love!

I haven't met him or spoken to him over the phone in ages, but I want to know about him, think about him, and I love dreaming about us. It doesn't bother me what he thinks about me now, wherein his life he places me, and I have no expectations. I am happy with where I am and what he means to me. Whether I am still special to him does not worry me. Now, is this not love? An unconditional love that requires no words, yet has all the emotions and feelings.

Does this sound like your own story? Are your emotions for that special someone from the past still alive? Did this story remind you of someone capable of melting your heart? How wonderful to relive those moments in your heart and mind without letting anyone catch who you are dreaming about! That's the magic of unspoken words!

3

From Lovers to Friends

There are unsaid conversations between ex-lovers who are together in different situations. They realize the awkwardness and uneasiness between themselves, yet discussing or getting into the past is pointless.

Most of us have been there, in such situations where a simple greeting seems awkward, let alone a discussion of the past. The journey from lovers to exes is not an easy one, especially if your situation requires you to place them in the friend zone to make life uncomplicated.

We meet pretty often and discuss work, friends, and our day-to-day life with our respective partners and kids. She and I try to be as normal as we can, yet somewhere the past feelings resurface and I yearn to hold her hand while she continues to talk.

We pretend there was never ever anything between us, yet sometimes references to the past incidents take us back to the time when we were together—the happy and romantic couple who made promises of staying together forever, till death do us apart! What a joke it sounds now!

Life puts us in situations that force us to become outstanding actors. If nominated for awards, we can unquestionably win loads for best acting and best smiles. During our family get-togethers, we act like two super lucky families dining together, our kids are inseparable when they meet, and our partners do not have the slightest idea of our past relationship and that makes me uneasy sometimes.

What if our secret gets out? How would everyone take that? How would they reflect on us? These questions often make me wonder if staying apart and not mixing families was a better idea. Why did we involve the families? We could have stayed friends who work together and often meet after work for drinks and dinner with other colleagues.

The unsaid language of love is often visible on our faces when we see each other with our families. Some jealousy and some hopelessness creep in. This could have been us if we married— this unfulfilled dream never leaves me.

It is both a pleasure and a difficult situation staying around her; it feels wonderful when she is around, and it is uncomfortable when she is missing in the picture. She is like an addiction I can't get rid of. Both of us are much committed to our partners and we are extremely responsible parents, too, but love understands nothing. It plays with your emotions, forcing your mind to intervene and handle the situation most of the time.

She is an extraordinarily dedicated and committed partner and a parent. I can't deny comparing her to my wife or not fantasizing about her when making love to my partner. I don't know if she does the same because her actions and gestures say nothing about how she feels about me and the whole situation of us working together and meeting with our respective families.

There is a possibility, she too, thinks about me when she is in bed with her husband; maybe she gets jealous also when she sees me with my wife. There are unsaid boundaries drawn between us to keep matters uncomplicated, but there are no defined boundaries in your mind; you are free to think and create scenes that only you follow and admire. I am happy to make love to her in my mind, to hold her, kiss her, and imagine a life with her.

Nobody can control or steal my thoughts; I am free to enjoy and imagine everything I want to. I wish the best for her and her family, but there is no shame in admitting that if given a chance, I would rather choose her as my life partner than a friend!

4

Childhood Love

In his eyes, I saw love and only pure love. I never felt like this for anyone, and I don't remember anyone else adoring and yearning for me. It seemed pure; it looked real. I was going with the flow, almost following my heart and ignoring everything that could alter my feelings and make me suspect otherwise. I felt like the chirpy little bird whose happiness and excitement were inexplicable.

The fantasy world, where I lived with my beloved, had everything needed to live a happy life; the imaginary love-making and lip locks would make me blush and put a smile on my face.

My trips to college and cafes would never be alone. I always had the company of my best friend, my beloved. From school to college, years passed by but we remained together; it became much easier to plan my life ahead with this special someone, for I had no doubts or questions about settling down with my childhood love. But higher education required both of us to find a decent college and move out of our comfort zones.

We moved to different parts of another city for our master's programs. It was fate that kept us together, in the same city, but different colleges, many miles away. Physically, we lived miles apart and met each other every weekend, but in our hearts, we were inseparable and just a call away.

Distance makes the heart grow fonder—ever heard this quote? Well, it's a lie. Distance doesn't make you love anyone more; it only brings more distance—between our hearts and phones. We started ignoring each other's calls, each other's company.

We tried to accept that it's just a phase and we still want to be together, but in our hearts, we had created a distance. Amidst life and college, highs and lows, there were phases when we missed the friendship we once shared. Telephonic conversations were the only solution convenient for us. We often helped each other stay motivated to earn good grades, but as time passed, priorities changed.

The decision to continue this failed relationship for the sake of childhood love looked unjustified and forced. We had given up on each other.

We called it off. Yes, we did. The fairy tale story ended with a rather surprising end; most of our friends couldn't accept and understand what went adrift between the most lovable and inseparable couple. So, how did we fall apart? If you ask me, I don't exactly know the correct answer, but I guess I was enjoying the recent developments in my life—new friends, attention, and a lively college environment.

Keeping the spark alive in the old relationship meant giving up the new acquaintances and friendships, parties, and post-college meetups and clinging on to him for anything or everything. The label 'taken' or 'committed' was not something I wanted against my name.

The fun, entertainment, and adventure that my new buddies brought in was the missing element in my relationship. From new relations to new friends, my idea of life had transformed completely; I preferred to experience this phase than remain caught in the former one.

I was glad I wasn't the one to break this news—we both fell

out of love gradually and understood it; both of us acknowledged it, too. But we were wise; we chose to keep the friendship alive and give our relationship another shot when it seemed right.

It's been fifteen years and we are still together. After all that we went through, amidst all the self-created chaos in our hearts and minds, we concluded childhood love is the best. It was our best decision to stick around together.

The freshness of the impressive college life faded rapidly; the mirror of life exposed the honest side of newly-formed friendships, relationships, and people in diverse situations. We stood by each other as friends through thick and thin; we were present when nobody was.

Dating wasn't the criteria for us to be together—that's the charm of strong bonds. Distance made us part ways but for a short while; it made us understand who we genuinely are when the right person stands by us.

What did we learn from our experience? We learned never to give in to the momentary shifts in any relation and that certain matters of the heart only time can settle. What we do not understand now becomes self-explanatory when the time is right. So, cheers to the couples staying strong and good luck to those still discovering their path in the journey called love!

5

Dreaming about the Perfect Love Story

"A heart without dreams is like a bird without feathers!" —Suzy Kassem

Some dreams never leave you; some unfulfilled desires remain in your heart. While every relationship is special and brings with it immense joy and new experiences, what we truly desire and dream about never leaves us.

Years later, the unfulfilled desires resurface and make us dream about the perfect relationship, the perfect love story we never had. Imaginary life situations and an overabundance of love cover most of such dreams.

So, what if we couldn't have the perfect love story in actual life, the imaginary, dreamy world of the most pious and fulfilling love stories live in our heart! We can live it whenever we like; we can feel it and nobody would know. It makes us happy and nobody is jealous; we can hold on to it and nobody would question. Isn't this amazing? There is nobody to question our sanity for believing in and following who we truly love.

There are hundreds of perfect life situations, incidents, and stories that dominate most of my dreams. I often lay in my bed and dream about returning to the early years when love was sharing a cup of coffee with your lover in your favorite cafe, sitting at the coziest table in the corner. Love was teasing each other, making future plans, wedding plans, and dreaming about having a smooth, wonderful life that had nothing to worry about. Dreams always have perfect stories—zero problems, no issues, and minor struggles. That's the reason they are dreams, not actual life. There is no harm in pleasing your own self by dreaming about those endless love stories that make you feel loved, wanted, and cherished by your favorite person.

The best love stories are the ones you create in your mind and dream about every night. You never know when those dreams can turn into reality! So, don't stop dreaming, let nothing stop you from believing in love, in the perfect relationships. Amongst the millions of love stories, yours should be your favorite one!

'A true love story never ends!'

6

He Won Me Over with His Love

Do you ever have those days when love is the only emotion you feel? Someone takes the top seat in your head and you no longer understand anything about anyone else? Do you ever experience a peculiar pain in your heart when someone leaves you for a short while? Some days love is the king. It drives your mind and soul and you blindly follow the footsteps shown to you toward your soulmate.

The last few days have seen me high on emotions. There is something more intense than love for him, inexplicable, but heartfelt, passionate, and enjoyable. I keep looking at his picture in his absence, smell his cologne to imagine his presence, hug the pillow tight as I have him in my arms, and wait for us to be together in bed. It looks like love has taken over me altogether. I am head over heels for him.

Last night, we lay in bed, close to each other. Our fingers

intertwined as we locked hands, gazing at the ceiling and sometimes looking into each other's eyes while we talked about our heartfelt emotions for each other, feelings that have transformed to become stronger since the time we met.

He took a deep breath and used both his hands to frame my face as his lips moved closer to mine, "*I have always loved you. I still do!*" His deep, passionate voice sent shivers down my spine. I noticed a current flow through my body. I wrapped my arms around him to hug him tightly, and a long kiss followed before I could express my feelings for him that had gone from deep to deeper.

I wanted to keep him in my arms all night long. It was cozy and warm with him. When you are in love, you experience various emotions that give you a fresh perspective of yourself and the one you love.

To put my sentiments in words was a bit intriguing, but I knew his heart would melt if I opened up to speak my mind. So, I smiled, gathered some courage, and looked directly into his eyes:

"*I have never felt so deeply for you, just the thought of not having you around kills me. You have completely taken over my mind. Like a teenage girl in love, I dream about you making love to me and I imagine you near me wherever I go."*

I paused and took a deep breath.

"Your effect on me is truly magical!" I giggled as I cuddled him so his face touched mine and his breath blew across my face.

It surprised him to hear some expressions of love from me. His smile broadened as he moved closer to me and tucked a curl behind my ear.

"I kept my promise, I told you I will make you crazy for me and I did it. I am happy you realized what I went through each time I had to let you go and why I was always desperate to get a glimpse of you and hold you tight in my arms. Now you understand how much it hurts to be away from the one you love." I smiled and kissed him, *"I love you."*

He proved it right. I never loved him enough until I got married to him. He was the one who chased me, proposed to me, and convinced me to marry him. The magic of his charm was hard to ignore; his true gentleman style was very impressive and attractive. A perfect match with a good compatibility score!

He not only loved me but was quite mature to make the right decisions, not to forget how settled he was, unlike most guys I had recently met. His frequent trips to meet me, early in the day or late at night, either at my workplace or at my home, said much about what I meant to him. It wasn't difficult to sense his love for me and the importance he gave to our relationship.

I had developed some kind of affection for him, but I wasn't as crazy in love as he was for me. He had once told me it was love at first sight for him and he just followed me, or shall I say stalked me to know me better. I remember how he proposed to me in his car, late at night. Nothing fancy, just a simple red rose, and in his deep voice, he said,

"I promise, one day you will fall deeply in love with me. Just marry me, please."

I guess he was right. I am now intensely in love with him, so much that I want to hold him tight in my arms forever. It is easier to understand his emotions now and relate to his random knocks on my door at odd hours just to see me. I show similar signs of anxiety and desperateness that he showed earlier. His company has definitely stirred up my emotions, making me want him even more.

I can easily profess my love for him now since we are on the same page—we share the same emotions and craziness for each other; we are insanely in love and our impassioned kisses have increased and become more public. Sometimes, love happens late in life, but when it happens, it makes you count your blessings and understand the true meaning of a soul mate. I am fortunate he persuaded me to marry him, and I trusted him when I took the life-changing decision. He is my Mr. Right!

7

In Love with a Married Man

There are days when you wonder why situations can't be easier and why plans can't be as smooth as they appear in our dreams. Why is it so hard to express feelings and even harder to get your love to love you back? I am in love with a tall, smart, and sexy senior colleague, who is married. I fell in love with him the day I met him at a team lunch and couldn't take my eyes off him. He was calmly sipping his white wine and showing off his knowledge with his excellent use of top-end vocabulary.

I was the nervous, fresh out of college, young girl, unfamiliar with team lunch etiquettes at this upscale restaurant with senior colleagues. Even the cutlery looked more expensive than my handbag. A team member introduced me to the senior colleagues at the lunch, most of whom were recognizable.

It was him I was meeting for the first time. He was a senior team lead, working with us on a need basis as he had several other teams to manage. He welcomed me with his firm handshake and looked straight into my eyes. His questions and conversation made me comfortable, and his way of including everyone in the conversation mesmerized me.

Is age a criterion for loving someone? I realize I am considerably younger than him, but does it really matter how old are you or what is the age difference between lovers? Does the 'married' label stop you from falling for someone else, someone much younger than you? I don't know what he thinks about me but I am crazy for him; I am always seeking ways to be around him.

It's this kind of madness that people my age can relate to. He is much more serious, balanced, and quiet; he doesn't seem to be as impatient and crazy as I am.

I have noticed him watching me when I am at my desk; he often looks at me and smiles. He has more than once asked me to have lunch together. Although this proves nothing, but my heart wants to believe that he loves me. Is his married status stopping him from coming closer to me? Is he holding back his feelings for me because he is committed to another woman who he calls his wife?

Friends have warned me against dating him since he is married, but how do I ask my heart to stop loving this man I cannot stop dreaming about? I yearn for him, my eyes are constantly looking for him, I find ways of going to his cubicle and talking to him; I know I am going crazy, but how do I stop it?

Is a single status necessary for liking someone and proposing to that someone? Do we need to be single to fall in love? Is falling in love with married men allowed? Do married people love singles and other married people or is love limited to a singles' club? I get that there are no rules in matters of the heart, but I agree I shouldn't go overboard with my emotions. Time is the key here. I must give myself time to determine how stable my heart is after a couple of months or a year.

It is possible that I reach nowhere with this love of mine, but I am happy that just him being around makes me content. I get a sense of gratification each time I see him. Someday, I will confess how much I love him and that I have zero expectations from him; I will love him even if he never loves me back. The unconditional love everyone talks about in books and movies, I guess I am already feeling it. This spirit, the love, and emotions, nobody can take away from me and I am so glad it happened to me.

Someday, he will know there is a girl out there who dreams about him, wants to be with him, and adores him. This may help him understand the depth of my love. Till then, let me sink in the feeling of one-sided love. I must wait until the feelings are mutual.

8

Love Finds You Behind the Doors, Too

They were not hickeys as everyone teased me about enjoying a lusty and passionate night with my husband. The perception of a joyous marriage and a romantic husband made friends jealous, while relatives cooked up their own bedroom stories.

The naughty smiles and cheesy questions by friends and relatives were tough to respond to since no one could see the truth, no one had the brains to go beyond their regressive mindsets, and for once spot the truth behind my quietness.

There was nothing fancy in our relationship, nothing romantic. Like normal couples, there was sex but forced. I was being tortured behind closed doors by the man I loved dearly.

After a lot of convincing and arguments, our parents had agreed to our wedding, only to realize they were never wrong in their opinion about him and his family. In my worst nightmare, I had not imagined my love hitting me behind the doors only because I was way more qualified than him. I am a doctor, an MD, and he could barely finish his MBBS.

We fell in love in college, while studying for our MBBS. I graduated and did my MD while he struggled to get his only degree. He realized academically I was better than him, yet he chose me; he once appreciated that my love for him was above my degree, but that did not stop him from prohibiting me from working at a hospital.

My only hope—his parents, watched him hit me with sticks and supported him in his decision to not let me step out of the house. My love had failed miserably. There was no hope, instead, suicidal thoughts blocked my decision-making. He had failed me and I had no reason to live, no strength to go back to my parents and tell them they were correct about him and his family.

An angel came to my rescue when no one bothered to offer

me water while they locked me up in my room. There was no one present at home, yet I continued to bang the door and cry for water; I was dying, but my life didn't matter to anyone. I heard someone entering the house and that gave me some hope.

The door unlocked and with half-closed eyes I noticed HIM, standing with a bottle of water in his hands. His eyes bulged out in shock. A pale, fragile me was on the floor with no strength in my body. Without saying a word, HE helped me drink some water, held me in his arms, and took me out of the house. I knew this man; he was my neighbor. I don't know how he came inside; I had no strength to ask him any question, but my heart asked me to trust this man.

HE took me to the hospital and called the police and my parents. My physical injuries and mental trauma didn't merely shock my parents. Their anger reached another level where they could kill my husband. HE stood by me throughout my recovery, took care of me, but never said a word. Like an angel, this man rescued me from the clutches of that cruel family. HE helped me file for divorce and got me back on my toes.

I started my job as a doctor at the same hospital, but my sessions with my therapist are not over. Mental trauma takes time to heal. In the meantime, my parents supported me unconditionally, and HE drops by every day at my work, doesn't leave without giving me a kiss, and I proudly call HIM my husband now.

Your first love may not make your perfect love story. Some layers require removal before you can see the truth with naked eyes. Don't fall in love, rise and shine and let no one in the name of love pull you down!

9

Love Is Never Lost

There are days when I am heartened by your fragrance everywhere around me. During those moments you seem so close, I can almost hug you and ask you—why did you leave me alone in this world? Is this your way of staying close and checking on me?

How does it feel to see me in such a vulnerable state? I die every day thinking about that unfortunate day when life failed to give you another chance, leaving me heartbroken and taking away my love. How I wish there was a way to erase it permanently from our life! I wish I had stopped you. Why didn't I?

I wish I could fight destiny and bring you back from heaven. I can give up my life to see you again, hold you, hug you, and tell you how much I love you and how much I miss you. There is no one I want to settle for but you.

Nothing consoles me when I miss you. I want you so badly that waking up every day seems like a task.

Your memories and thoughts keep me alive; it's a state of trance I wish to stay in. What is life without our loved ones? With you, I lost my zeal to live and move on! The permanent pause in my life doesn't seem to play; it's stuck where you left me all alone!

Every corner of the room reminds me of our little chitchats, our romance, and our plans. The home that we built with love and memories doesn't appear like home anymore. I ask myself, why did it have to end like this?

My dreams are all shattered, my love is lost, and I am standing in between nowhere, thinking of what to do with my life. Time has stood still for me since the day you left; it's hard to distinguish between day and night. A part of me died with you when death took you away and gave me a permanent partner—pain!

I live in a whimsical world where just the two of us exist, living together as a happy couple, and no power can separate us. I see you are there for real, holding me tight. Now, I will not let you leave me heartbroken and alone. You are mine and forever mine. But I see you are slowly freeing yourself and moving away. Why? As you reach the window, you wave goodbye to me and disappear into the light. Where did you go? Why did you leave me again? Your fragrance faints and the signs of your presence become dull. Are you gone forever? I have nothing left except my tears and they seem to give me no hope.

I sit by the window of my 17th-floor apartment and peek outside. Maybe my life is over, my days here are done; I should be where you are. We will meet once again in heaven and stay together forever. This could put an end to my restless wandering, taking me a step closer to you. I looked outside the big, wide window of my living room.

 The fast-running cars appear tiny from the high-rise; the pedestrians are barely visible. I stuck my head out of the window to look at death, calling out my name. The distance between my window and the ground looked scary, but my mind knew what it wanted.

Before I could lean a little more to take the extreme step I had been contemplating since your death, a certain force pulled me back and pushed me on the floor in anger. I fell down with my eyes wide open in bewilderment. What just happened? Was it you? Did you throw me down on the floor? You stopped me from taking my life!

I realized you were here. I knew you wouldn't leave me alone. With a smile on my face, I closed the window and wiped my tears. There is peace in my heart because I can once again sense your presence; your fragrance is back. You are close to me, back in your house. Even with no words, I can hear you, have you around. You will forever be mine; stay here, our story isn't complete!

10

We Share a Special Bond

We were laughing so hard, holding our bellies, that at one point, the spectators thought we were crazy, but it didn't matter because we were so happy. I don't remember the reason we were laughing so much. Maybe, it was each other's company.

We were usually happy together, and we liked to enjoy and have fun, but that day, it was something else. It had never happened before. The laughter caused the soda we were drinking to flow out of our noses, and we almost fell out of the car holding our bellies.

Did you ever laugh your lungs out before a bunch of strangers? Well, here we were, carefree souls, laughing our hearts out, not caring much about the onlookers! Imagine the happiness someone brings into your life!

We made a stop at The Tea Shop—the very popular cafe where youngsters hung out. The owner had only one condition—no ruckus and no noise; he was a military veteran, thus the whole discipline angle while we were just having fun. He noticed our loud giggles and his stern eyes immediately signaled to keep our voices low, but we ignored him.

"Looks like you two are high on something? Why do you need tea after drinking too much?" Our laughter suddenly stopped and my surprised look made the owner's eyes bulge out. Leaving the cafe sounded more preferable since getting thrown out by the lieutenant would be too embarrassing. If his temper wasn't an issue, my response would have been,

"Yes, we are high, on jokes and awesome company." I am sure he wouldn't have appreciated my answer.

Being together meant fun, entertainment, and too many conversations. It always felt great and bright. A certain fondness, unexpressed love, and attraction tied our friendship. We were slightly more than friends and a little less than lovers who enjoyed spending time together, indulged in fun activities, and loved eating out. Like a couple, we would fight and makeup, but we were not lovers.

I don't know if I should call it dating because when we were not together, we would talk over the phone or chat online. We tried to portray ourselves as just colleagues at our workplace, but could not fool everyone. People could see our mutual admiration, our color-matching schemes every day, and our flirtatious ways when one of us passed by. For us, the office was more about healthy flirting than friendship.

We could have gone ahead with our friendship to convert it into a romantic relationship, but we didn't. Some relationships do not need a label. That way we could avoid any complications, keep the expectations low, and not entangle the emotional strings. We cared for each other, but love was a complicated, unspoken chapter that neither one of us wished to hop on.

It's been over ten years now. Both of us are married and settled in our respective lives, but whenever we talk, we flirt just like before. We can still crack jokes and laugh like crazy; it is still fun to be together. A friend once told me— not every relationship should end in marriage. Few relationships are meant for memory's sake, to remind you of the joy and ecstasy a special person brings into your life.

This piece of advice has stayed with me.

You will always be one of my fondest memories, one I will always cherish and laugh and smile about. You can uplift my mood in seconds and even though we barely talk, whenever we do, I become the younger version of myself, always trying to be naughty, flirty, and forever young!

Thanks for creating those special moments with me, they are the reason I am so fond of you; they keep us connected and remind us of the wonderful past that was special in its own way!

11

Distance Makes the Heart Grow Fonder

It wasn't a simple decision for us. To focus on our careers and growth prospects and leave the love aside. Long distance wasn't for us. We were not prepared for it and we didn't want to force each other to stay committed to a relationship with frequent phone calls and messages.

Yes, we agreed to stay friends and observe how distinct elements affect our relationship in a few years and see how well we cope with this separation. It was a hard decision, and that moment when we agreed on having an open relationship with no strings attached is engraved in my memory forever.

We were young, and we were both ambitious. Being stuck in a long-distance relationship was not something we imagined. Hence risking our careers for this relationship made no sense. Some decisions are hard and this was one of those decisions that you take and regret a thousand times only to realize you cannot fall weak before circumstances.

The fast-moving workplace in a foreign land looked promising, but amidst hard-working professionals, that missing smile and a familiar face was all I needed to make me feel comfortable. It felt lonely to not have someone sit next to you, someone who cares and looks out for you. There was nobody waiting for me in the cafeteria. I was lonely, awfully lonely.

A few weeks passed with me sulking and crying. I questioned how long I was going to stay in this miserable state and to what extent I would let it affect me. To move ahead by making new friends was the only solution; I challenged myself to stop waiting for that familiar face and smile to come and help me put myself together.

I had enough of the lies on phone calls and in messages, I had to set matters right for myself. This was another decision that I presumed would change my life.

New friends, parties, and frequent hangouts after work

kept me busy during the day. I would check out new girls and try to be friends with them, but somewhere I missed her, her smile, and innocence. I didn't want to let her know how miserable I was without her, hence I made deliberate attempts of replying late to her sweet, lovey-dovey messages and phone calls. It was my way of telling her *'how well I am without you.'*

She was acting weird, too. She wouldn't take my calls or give timely replies to my messages during the day. At night, she would give me an excuse of going to bed early because of morning meetings.

It was evident she had found someone else and was busy chatting with the other guy. Her behavior made me uncomfortable and anxious. How could she move on so early? I couldn't complain since we were no more tied to each other. I craved to confront her, but I had no power to do so. She was no longer mine.

Love can be strange at times. You think it's over, yet it is far from over. The memories never die; they bring back the same emotions and feelings you once held, especially the hurt. Happiness can be forgotten, but hurt stays with you forever. Tears are a reminder of how badly you miss someone.

Sometimes, we wonder why life gets too complicated and why we can't get a straightforward way out and make situations benefit us. I had periods of hate and of love; I was trying to get over her until I spotted her at a store during my vacation in my hometown. She was visiting, too. What a coincidence! A little hesitant, but confident, I approached her with a broad smile on my face and stood right in front of her.

"Oh my, God! Look who is here!" She was amazed to see me. Her big broad smile looked natural. Her warm and long hug moved me to tears, I couldn't control myself and squeezed her in my arms.

"I missed you so much," I said.

She moved back from my shoulders, wiped her tears, and looked into my eyes. Then, she spoke.

"I missed you more than you can imagine."

"Really? Why no texts or calls then?" I asked.

She lowered her eyes to avert my gaze, and in a soft tone said, *"I was trying to get over you."*

Her reply made me look into her watery eyes, and a long

pause followed.

"Well, I, too, can't seem to settle without you in my life. Not a single day has passed without missing you. Can we be together again? It's not warm without you, it's lonely, very lonely," I said.

She nodded her head in agreement as tears rolled down her cheeks. Before I could wipe them, she was back in my arms, giving me a bear hug,

"I love you. I know I haven't expressed my feelings in a long time, but I really love you, and I have loved no one other than you."

We had forgotten that we were in a store where our love story was getting back on track. People stared at us, kids were shocked, and the store owner smiled while wiping her tears with a tissue. She had been a sole witness of our relationship since the beginning, till this day. It wasn't hard for her to understand what was going on between us.

What an amazing journey I have had with this wonderful lady! Seventeen years to our reunion at the store, and she continues to mesmerize me and holds the key to my heart. Our long distance ended shortly after this reunion as I changed my job to be closer to her. We still discuss our separation stories and boast of our commitment to each other; those very moments of reunion continue to spark our married life.

12

The Closure

I was sitting in Starbucks, working on a presentation for the next day. It was a boring day, and I took a break to browse Facebook to help me unwind.

A message from an old friend who had migrated to Canada a few years ago, brought sweet memories of my incomplete love story. She connected with me on social media after many, many years. We were together in school and lost touch after she moved to Canada with her family. In those days, without online platforms, it was difficult to keep in touch. I accepted her friend request and the first question she asked me was,

"So did you marry your girlfriend from school? You guys were so serious. How's she?" Her question left me numb. Almost twenty years and she remembers the very passionate love story I left behind long ago. I had no

answer to her question. I replied, *"Hey! You have some memory! Unfortunately, I am not in touch with her and have no clue where she is."* She said sorry, and we moved on to talk about Canada, her life there, kids, etc.

While I was chatting with her, I kept asking myself if I should look for the only girl I ever loved. Facebook might help. I began searching for her name, but there were hundreds of profiles that popped up. A lot changes in twenty years. She might have changed her name after the wedding or must have moved to some new city or country.

I knew nothing about her; I never kept in touch. But there was a girl who resembled her. She looked mature and much hotter than my girl. I wasn't sure, however, the name of the school we attended, and a few other details matched. Shall I send a friend request or write a message?

There were a few seconds of self-analysis and then I wrote a simple message:

"Hi! How are you? Long time...how have you been?" [Message Sent.] If she replies, it's her.

In less than a minute, she replied, *"As if you care!"* I smiled with joy because it was her. This used to be her typical reply in school. She seemed mad at me, even after all these years. Well, if she treated me like I treated her years ago, I would have never replied to her message.

"I understand that I upset you. I am sorry for what I did. Where are you? Can we meet or talk?" [Message Sent].

She sent me her phone number. *"Call me anytime. I am in the same time zone as you."*

This didn't explain if she would joyfully take my call or if she wanted to settle some score with me. But it proved she knew where I lived.

Well, since I was at fault, I accepted her tantrums and rudeness, and with shaky fingers, I dialed her number. I wasn't confident at all; I wasn't the same cool guy she once loved. The flashback of our love story appeared before my eyes as I waited for her to pick up my call.

"Hello," her voice had some maturity.

"Oh hi! This is..."

"I know who this is. How are you?" she asked.

"I am very well. How are you?" I asked her.

"I am alive and happy if that's what you wanted to find

out.”

The sarcasm in her tone wasn't what I was expecting, but it only proved how upset she was because I never kept in touch after moving to another country for higher studies. I never included her in my decision-making, got busy dating other girls, and didn't answer her calls. Her rudeness and anger were well-justified.

"I realize I upset you and I am sorry for everything.” I took a deep breath. *"Can we put the past behind us and talk about the present?”*

She wasn't that warm, but I got her to talk and open up about her current life. A successful career, loving husband, and two kids— she was doing fine in her life, but something was missing in her tone or maybe I was overanalyzing.

We started messaging and talking about every few days and she started laughing at my jokes. My family saw a livelier man who came home with a big smile, and she sounded happier, too, unlike our first phone call.

Months later, I had a professional conference in the city she lived in and I couldn't be happier attending it with the sole purpose of meeting her. We set up our meeting in the same hotel where I was staying after my conference was over. I planned to stay one extra night after the conference to spend time with her and asked her to meet me in the dining hall of the hotel.

There she was, entering the hotel, dressed in a shimmery black dress and her silky, smooth hair flowing in the air. She stood apart from the rest of the crowd and I had a flashback of all the wonderful times we shared while dating. I told myself, *"She could have been mine if I had not done the silly act of ditching her."*

She mesmerized me with her charisma and for a moment, I forgot about my wife and kids. It was difficult to take my eyes off her, and I had to remind myself she belongs to someone else.

"You look so pretty!"

"Thanks," she said.

We hugged like long-lost friends. I wanted her to stay in my arms forever and kiss her as lovers do, but my silly mistake had put me in this situation. Swallowing the truth, I pulled out the chair for her and got ready for our very formal dinner. I guess talking over the phone was much better than meeting her in person. She was formal and she was pretty, both of which were quite distracting.

"*Shall we go to some other place after dinner? Somewhere more casual, where we can be ourselves and talk more openly?*" I asked her, and she agreed.

But I realized it was late, and I had limited knowledge of the city, so I asked her if she would like to sit in my suite for coffee. She was so formal that I thought she would say no, but she agreed. We proceeded to my suite, and I ordered coffee for both of us.

"*Please make yourself comfortable. Don't be shy.*" She smiled and nodded in agreement.

She sat on the couch while I took off my jacket and hung it in the closet. I sat next to her and looked into her eyes; she also looked at me. A little unsure of what I wanted to say, I gathered the courage to apologize to her.

"*I am sorry for what happened between us. It was my fault and I am sorry for not keeping in touch with you. To be honest, I had no courage to face you. I regret letting you go, and if there is one part I can change, it would be the time I went ahead, leaving you behind. If given a chance, I would fix my mistakes, reverse the time to move back to where we started, and never leave you. I know it's not a possibility, but I wanted to give closure to our relationship that never took off in its proper sense. And I am the one responsible for it. I am extremely sorry.”*

My teary eyes felt this moisture after ages, but it felt satisfying to lighten my heart with an apology that she deserved. Her moist eyes kept looking at me as I wiped my tears and held her hand. It is possible she was awaiting an explanation since I left her, until today; it was the much-deserved closure she was expecting for so long.

 She came closer, held my face with both her hands, and kissed me on my lips. I reciprocated by kissing her back and indulged in the passionate lip lock as if this was the final step in the closure story. We got closer, and I was almost leaning on her, my hands on her back as her breasts pressed against my chest. I reluctantly moved my hands on her back and tried to unzip her dress, but she pushed me back as if she just woke up from a scary dream.

“We must stop, we are both married.”

Embarrassed by my act, I looked at her in agreement and moved away from her on the couch.

“Sorry, I didn’t mean to…”

“It’s okay. I started…” she said.

She got up, fixed her dress and her hair, and grabbed her handbag from the table, ready to leave. *"I should go. It's already too late."*

"No, stop, please. I know we shouldn't have kissed, but could you stay a little longer? We can go for a walk." I couldn't make up any other reason for her to stay.

She was standing at the door, trying to avoid any eye contact. *"It's best to leave now and not spoil what's left between us. I shall keep in touch. You take care and have a safe flight back home."*

I saw her leave, and I had no right to stop her. I closed the door and lay in the bed, thinking of the kisses and our intimacy. There was happiness and some disappointment. I could still feel her soft skin on my face and smell her floral fragrance. I was going into deep sleep thinking about her when my phone rang. Believing it would be her, I grabbed it from the table. It was my wife and kids, asking me about my flight details.

The call reminded me of my family that is waiting for me; it was a reminder of the past that cannot become present. The time we left behind and our present cannot mingle.

She was correct when she left, a minute more, and we

would have ruined our present lives and families.

It's been five years. I didn't see her again. We often exchange texts and greetings on occasions, but nothing more than that. She has a permanent spot in my heart, but sadly she needs to be there in a dormant state. That's best for both of us. My little cheating is still under wraps and I am happy my family has no clue about it.

HURT

Heartbreaks are hard but a part of life; they help you realize the importance of loyalty, stability, and love in a relationship!

1

It All Came Back to Me

We were young lovers, still in high school, but not completely mastering the meaning of love, yet expressing it every day by saying the famous three words—*I love you!* School love is special.

The unfamiliarity with the initial experiences of the chemical interaction in the brain causes vivid dreams; it makes you believe in love and how it is above everything else. Because everything is unfamiliar and every emotion is fresh, heartbreaks are more painful and delicate to handle.

I didn't realize I was breaking his heart; I didn't realize my decision of moving away from his life would shatter him.

It was the teenage life of high dreams, ambitions, fun, and romance. The thought about settling with one person suffocated me; I chose to enjoy the thrill of a young age that had just begun. He, being the conservative lover, would dream about nothing but me. His ambitions were nothing but staying close to me. His love had sadly become too clingy. The freedom I desired seemed too much to ask for; he couldn't support my dreams and I couldn't become a committed partner. We parted ways or I should say I left him.

Shocked and shattered, he tried to confront me several times, but each time I would avoid him. I didn't wish to reveal to him I no longer liked him, that I wanted a better world, or I preferred to stay single. His frustration and anger were always visible on his face and he must have unquestionably cursed me several times.

The love had turned into resentment and hatred, too, but I didn't care. Staying away from him didn't make a difference in my life. I had obviously moved on.

Love touched me afresh, but this time it was someone mature and not a teenage boy. He was a guy in his twenties, a working professional who proposed to me and after a few dates, I fell in love with him. This gentleman did not have the aggression of a teenage boy, no impulsive behavior; he was gentle, confident, and possessed the wisdom and experience of communicating with young ladies like me. Quite a charmer, he was!

Love was different with him, for there was no college romance, no love letters, no cards. It was only phone calls and face-to-face meetings. We met every day and also talked over the phone, not for hours since he was a working man, but our late-night phone calls would be naughty and adult. He made me feel like a woman and not a college girl; he would treat me like a partner and share his life goals with me. No matter how mature he was, I wasn't mature enough to deal with separation when he moved to another country for further studies. From his age and profession, I didn't think he would study any further. He left me with a lot of promises of phone calls and emails.

It was a different time with no internet or WhatsApp calls. I was a student with no mobile phone or sufficient money for international calls, but my pocket money helped me call him every few weeks for a few minutes.

My love for him was strong, but despite my efforts, the long-distance relationship could not survive for long. My ex-boyfriend seemed to have cursed me, and this curse ruined the relationship. He left me the way I left my school love; he wouldn't answer me, just like I didn't answer the boy.

My calls and emails went unanswered, exactly like I did some time back. So, it was all coming back to me now. I realized I was being punished for breaking someone's heart, for not giving closure to the relationship. The betrayal was an eye-opener of the pain I caused to my young lover, of how it must have impacted him when I refused to talk or listen to him.

I experienced the pain of emptiness and despair; I knew somewhere my ex must be peaceful because I am broken now. No matter how hard I tried to win my love, he would not come back. I tried to get over him and move on, but the pain of not knowing why someone betrayed me still was disturbing. It was a reminder of what I did to the young lover; I received what I once did! It felt like a full circle— what goes around, comes around!

This relationship taught me why closure is important in any broken relationship. To leave someone with no answers is brutal; the truth may hurt, but it is better than leaving someone wondering about what they did wrong in the relationship. I received the fruits of my *karma*, and I am still learning to make peace with the breakup!

2

How to Describe YOU?

Hanging out at our favorite coffee shop with friends and solving Sudoku puzzles was my favorite after-class activity. That day, we skipped the last period to hang out at the cafe and plan a night out or movie over the weekend.

While everyone was debating movie night, I was texting back and forth, trying to set up a dinner date with HIM. I was smiling and typing and also sipping coffee in between my texts. A friend interrupted my messaging to ask me a question that nobody had ever asked. She asked me to describe YOU and tell everyone how the interaction between us turned magical and transformed into a relationship.

Considering how popular you were among the girls, everyone's prince charming and a dream date, I sensed some kind of jealousy in the question. I beamed and blushed, thinking about how lucky I am to have you in my life.

Before I could begin describing you, I closed my eyes and saw your face smiling at me. My friend snapped her fingers to interrupt my dream, and I opened my eyes with a big smile on my face.

"He is brilliant, charming, bright, caring, and has a multi-faceted personality. He is every girl's dream, a fantasy they would love to explore; even other men are jealous of him. To date him is a matter of high pride for any girl, and I consider myself really special with him."

There were claps from my friends who couldn't help laughing at my description of my boyfriend. I played along and laughed with them.

I may have laughed along with my friends over my description of you, but I meant every word I said. If I think about you and your charisma around girls at college, I had not dreamed about dating you in my wildest dreams; I was too ordinary to imagine a boyfriend like you. Your performance at the college concert blew my mind, and I was already dreaming about spending my life with you. Why you walked up to me and talked to me after the concert still makes my friends jealous.

"So, were you all jealous when he talked to me and not you all?" I asked my friends.

Their mischievous smiles and nodding heads were telling me a different story. I know for a fact that it surprised everyone to see me with the most happening guy in college, considering how average I look. There was gossip about what strings I pulled to attract him.

Well, it doesn't matter now. What matters to me is that you noticed me in the huge college crowd and came to chat with me. Our meetings became so frequent that sometimes my favorite coffee shop would see me twice a day—first with friends and then with you.

Our relationship had moved from being 'casual' to 'committed' a little too soon. The way you controlled my decisions and actions appeared normal in the beginning; your little possessiveness also made me feel loved and wanted; your idea of always holding hands at public places and while strolling around gave me a sense of security. What else could a girl ask for in a relationship?

Well, this was all in the past. The all-fancy, rosy relationship soon faded, shade by shade. A lot changed in a few months that followed the coffee shop conversation with friends. My views about you and our relationship changed drastically.

Your little gestures, habits, and thoughts started bothering me a little too much. Every minor act seemed more like an invasion of privacy; I realized the right to live an easy, independent life is more important than staying in a relationship with a partner killing you slowly.

The world was jealous of seeing us together, but this togetherness was killing me inside; I wanted to breathe and get your hands off me. The more time I spent with you, the urge to break up with you became stronger. It was choking; I was sinking, and my friends could sense some trouble in my behavior.

The coffee shop became more like an explanation spot, where I would constantly explain to you my situation over the phone or in person. The Sudoku puzzles would go untouched. My buddies wanted to help but you never let them intrude; you kept them away from me, from us. I would be a liar if I denied the immense hatred that I had developed for you, for always keeping a check on me, not letting me do what I wished to do; you took away my freedom while you continuously flirted with other girls.

Someone I trusted sensed my deteriorating mental health and came to my rescue; I would like to call him my savior. This special someone not only gave me the courage to be strong and break up with you but also held my hand when I was all broken inside. I quit the suffocating relationship that offered no windows to breathe.

This special someone is my present partner, the one who pulled me out of that turmoil.

He went crazy when I left him to be with my savior. Many blamed me for his disturbed mental state after the breakup, but it doesn't matter to me what people think and speak. Nobody saw my tears when I was choking in his over-possessive love; I was dying, and nobody could help.

Today, I feel happy and blessed to be out of that traumatic relationship that would have led me to a mental asylum. I am a free bird now that can fly wherever she likes, live life on her terms; there is much emphasis on trust and respect in my new relationship. I am no longer treated as private property that anyone can claim whenever they like.

So, what shall I say to describe YOU? I don't want to malign your image, but I have nothing much to say about your fake, dominating, possessive nature. You were a bad dream, a nightmare, and I am glad it's all over between us!

3

You Left Me Because You Wanted To

You are not the type of person I would choose to date or spend my life with, yet you intrigue me with your charm. There is something about your dark looks and deep eyes that pulls me to you.

Your conversations are so interesting to keep everyone glued to and wanting more of them; you ignore me in a way that I notice is for the world. Deep inside I know you like me. Despite the conflicts and disagreements, I am more than willing to forget and put our troubled past behind us and continue to be friends.

But each time you repeat your version of what went wrong in our relationship, and why we couldn't be together, no matter how convincing your answers are, my instinct is that you weren't that courageous then.

No matter how much you expressed your love and attraction for me, back in college, it was you who gave up and walked away. It was you who had no courage to get into a relationship with me and now you talk about your heroism. Sorry, but it sounds fictional to me.

You keep justifying your actions and giving random reasons for moving away from me as if it matters now. You did what you needed to do; there is nothing you can do to change it or prove that it was right. And making me part of your wrong decisions will do no good to you. Holding me partly responsible for what you did to me ages ago justifies nothing. If you had the courage, we would be together today.

To tell me you moved apart because you didn't want to upset a friend who liked me, too, doesn't make you a martyr. Love means sacrificing for your close ones, but this was stupidity. I wish you had asked me once what I wanted instead of conveniently closing your doors on me. What kind of a lover does that? Your love was never strong enough to push you to stand up for yourself.

I strongly feel your story is something you made up just

like your lame excuses. You have nothing left to repeat or explain, and possibly you are once again attracted to me, so a fake story would help gain sympathy. But I got over you sooner than I hoped and became the stronger person I am today, that can't be fooled easily. I am no more the naïve person who would believe everything you say. The only advantage you have is our short but beautiful past. There was a time I loved you, so regardless of your lies, cheating, and false stories, I don't hate you.

It does hurt to not have you in my life, but it's good that we parted our ways long ago, and it would be best if we never talk. Irrespective of how strong I may portray myself, the truth is that I am still attracted to you; you continue to haunt my thoughts and I don't understand why the wrong ones always look right!

4

The Big Regret of Life

I still regret not answering your calls on my big day, the day of my wedding. I was unaware of your thoughts, feelings, and what you were going through then, but I realized you were desperate to talk to me. Ten missed calls! That definitely meant something. I still wonder what I missed by not answering your calls.

My phone was constantly ringing, and I saw your name flashing on my screen, but I didn't want to talk to you. No, there wasn't any reason for ignoring your calls. I was getting ready for my big day; amidst anxiety and nervousness, I couldn't care much about a phone call.

Answering the phone and listening to your congratulatory talk wasn't important for me then. I was happy because I was starting afresh—a new life, a different journey with my prince charming. Like every bride, I preferred to look beautiful and get photographed from every angle. A phone call was a low priority for me.

When the freshness of the wedding faded, I thought about you and your call on my big day. What if I had taken your call? What would have changed? Would you have confessed your feelings for me, apologized to me, or simply asked me to elope with you because you still loved me but married someone else? I have no clue, and I didn't care then when I decided not to take your call. I don't know if it was a wise choice.

But today, I regret that decision. I wish I could have listened to what you had to say, even if it was a mere congratulatory call. But, ten missed calls only to congratulate? No. Seems you had something else on your mind.

I understand we were out of touch for a while after you got married. You were busy with your newly-wedded bride, enjoying the excitement and thrill of a new relationship. That also explains why I did not bother to share the news about my wedding with you early on.

I am unaware of how you felt when you heard about me entering the magical state of wedlock. The situation looked difficult to work out between us, but you quickly moved on without giving it a try. On your wedding day, you called me and acted as if everything was fine.

You portrayed a picture of the two of us with no feelings, no emotions. You pretended to be normal but taking out time to talk to me on a busy wedding day definitely meant something else.

There was something strange between us. The unexpressed frustration and feelings bothered me, but both of us acted well over the phone. I was happy for you; if I had expressed my feelings of any kind, they would have upset or confused you. Were you expecting me to ask you to pause and think about us?

No, that would have been immature and selfish, especially when you were embarking on a fresh journey. I was happy you were moving on, unlike me, stuck on you for no reason. You settled based on what you felt about me and the entire situation.

I believe you never attempted to work things out. You flew the simple route of finding a new partner and getting out of the complicated situation rather than resolving our matter. You expected 'moving on' by marrying someone else to be a smooth ride for you, but when reality bit, you turned to your old flame for the same warmth and comfort you expected from your new relationship.

Well, it was too late. I had taken a different path and married someone I saw had the courage to smooth out the tangled parts in any situation. He, unlike you, expressed his desire to marry me and spend his life with me.

Irrespective of how well settled we are in our respective lives, I am forever curious to rewind time and imagine what you would have expressed if I had answered your call on my wedding day! If I ask you, would you tell me, or is it too late for you to clarify that for me?

Ah! Why didn't I take your call? My most regretted decision so far!

5

I Lost Her Forever

Everyone has stories about breakups, bumping into a former crush, extramarital affairs, etc., but few carry stories where your ex-lover passes over to the other side of the realm and takes away any hopes of meeting again, any chances of ever telling them how much you loved them.

We lose the faint chances of getting back or fantasizing about them because they are no more alive. It is this void you cannot explain to anyone; it is this grief you cannot share. Life goes on and your inner feelings never get expressed; you learn to keep them suppressed in your heart because opening up and sharing is painful.

We, the inseparable couple, could not marry and settle down for reasons best left for history. It wasn't a simple decision, but moving on was the only solution. We sat on our favorite bench by the lake, holding hands while tears flowed from her eyes.

We made promises of never letting the past impede our future life. I was asking her to do something I realized was difficult, but I had to make sure she stayed happy in her married life. Being the stronger person didn't help; it tasted like a slow death.

I dropped her back at her apartment, and we made promises to stay away from each other. No phone calls, no messages, and no stalking. Of course, asking each other to not envision 'us' was not in our control. It was a hard stand, a deliberate one because moving ahead with your past doesn't help anyone.

We married our respective partners on the same date to avoid any inner, emotional turmoil, strong enough to force us to change our decision. The first year of marriage wasn't an easy one.

My wife's frustration and anger were visible in her actions and on her face as I tried little to connect with her. How could I talk to her about my lost love and the thought of adultery every time I touched her? I had to find a solution as my emotional baggage was affecting my married life. With this resolution in mind, I started planning a holiday with her.

My first ever trip with my wife had just begun when I received the terrible news from a friend. That phone call shook me. I stood there silent and numb and died a thousand deaths. It took me a while to absorb what I learned over the phone and then it hit me hard; I felt like screaming and crying and running to hug my beloved who passed away a few hours ago while delivering her newborn.

A shiver ran down my spine as I heard the tragic news of her untimely death. Trembling because of the shock, I gathered myself and told my wife that a dear friend has passed away and we needed to leave. She hugged me tight to support me and instantly started packing, but her question about 'who is it' did not get answered.

She sensed it was a female, someone very close because my tears didn't stop for a minute.

It took me a few hours to reach her place, and I saw her husband struggling with the newborn along with a few other women. I looked at her as her body lay on the hard floor, wrapped in a white sheet with garlands and flowers all over her.

This was not how I ever imagined her; this was not how I

expected it would end. I wanted to pick her up and hold her in my arms and I wished something magical would wake her up. I wanted to tell her, *"Look, I am here, I will never leave you. Please come back."*

I cried like a baby and everyone around who didn't know me assumed I was a close relative. My friends consoled me and asked me to let go of her hand, but I didn't care about anyone. I didn't want to part from her. Her cold lifeless hand, devoid of emotions, seemed strange.

While my friends tried to cheer me up, I kept repeating, *"I lost her, I lost her."*

I refused to leave her place and requested to see the baby. My tears and my sad state concerned the relatives who were not sure of my identity. But someone agreed to take me to the room where the little angel was sleeping peacefully, unaware of her mother's demise.

She had an uncanny resemblance to her mom, bringing more tears to my eyes. An inner voice told me—in this baby, my love will always live. She hasn't left completely. I wished I could raise her daughter just the way she wished and always described. She was my angel, my hope; I craved to hug her and tell her what her mom meant to me if only

I could do so.

That was the worst day of my life. To accept you have lost your love forever is the most dreadful thought and emotion. It took me a year to accept her death and face the reality. I will forever be grateful to my wife for being the pillar of support in my healing process. For a wife, to accept and respect her husband's ex-girlfriend is tricky. Her acceptance and support helped me smile once again.

A part of me still misses her and cries for her. I visit her place often and meet her daughter, who reminds me of my love. Her little fingers hold my hand, just like her mom used to do. It is strange and quite unbelievable that she never cries and is always smiling around me, just like her mother. Her guardian angel seems to be watching us from heaven above and is content to see me spending time with her little girl.

Some mistakes in life make you regret them forever. Maybe leaving her, not keeping in touch, was a mistake. I visit our favorite place often and sit on the same bench and reflect on our last day together. That hand, those tears, the promises, they are all gone. I sit alone with memories of our beautiful past, waiting to be with her one day.

In this lifetime, we couldn't be together, but in my next birth, I wish to be with her forever and not compromise on a future without her. My life isn't the same and it will never be, but her daughter is a reminder that she is partly with me.

6

The Anguish

What do you call your childhood love affair that still affects you? Do you still recall the old love, hurt, betrayal, passion, kisses, and random behavior, or just the person you loved then? After a good twenty years, he still thinks I ditched him for no reason; he still holds grudges against me.

A father of two kids yet stuck on past love; someone he should have long forgotten but likes to keep a love and hate relationship with me!

We bumped into each other at our school alumni meeting I had no plans of attending. After some convincing by friends, I joined them for an evening filled with nostalgia and old faces. Little did I know about the awkward encounter with him—my school time boyfriend!

We met, and I greeted him like I would greet an old friend.

I was very casual with him as I ignored our past relationship pretending to be normal and easy, unlike him who was cold and not so friendly.

The awkwardness between us was quite clear to our other friends. I took his behavior as a sign of age since it was twenty years ago that I last met him, to be precise 19 years and 7 months. I ignored everything about him and focussed on the reason I was here.

The alumni meeting had many faces I had long forgotten. Networking and catching up was fun; our talks wouldn't end. So, we all headed to a nearby pub for more chitchat. While I didn't want 'him' to be part of it, he automatically got added to the group.

I was chatting with almost everyone and trying to avoid him since he had his eyes fixed on me. It became uncomfortable after a while, and I asked a friend if we could exchange seats to maintain distance from him.

"Are you trying to avoid me?" he asked me as I looked at him with a scared face.

I chuckled and looked down to avoid the gaze and said 'no.' But then, I stared at him and with a straight face told him how his constantly fixed gaze on me was making me uncomfortable.

"Well, you have grown into a beautiful lady and I can't help but look at you and reminisce the good old dating days," he smiled as if it well-justified his actions.

"Well, thank you. I see you, too, have worked hard on your body, quite muscular," I replied.

"Yeah! I remember you loved muscular guys back then. Don't know if they still attract you."

Oh my god! He has some memory. *"Yes. I still like muscular men and my fiancé is one with hot abs."* I tried to show off and indirectly told him I was engaged.

"Good for you, girl. That tells me you are still unmarried. So, what chance do I have now?" He looked so confident like he absolutely had a chance!

I was unprepared for this kind of conversation and did not know the appropriate way to answer or graciously exit the scene. I smiled, raised a toast, and started walking away.

He was fast enough to follow me and block my way by standing right in front of me. I looked at him, puzzled. He held my hand and forced me out of the pub to talk in the parking lot. It was so quick; I had no time to respond.

There was complete silence in the parking lot, unlike the madness that was inside. A frightened me wanted to scream and call somebody for help. I looked at him and he looked at me, his expressions changed to that of an angry man, holding a lot inside him.

With no clue what this hot-headed man could do, I was regretting my decision of attending the alumni meeting. He seemed he would explode any second.

His expressions were scary; his nostrils flared as he burst out, *"My life toppled when you dumped me and moved on. I couldn't concentrate on my studies and had to settle for a mediocre college because of the average score. You have no idea of my mental state after you left. Yes, we were teenagers, but that doesn't mean my feelings were any less. I loved you and I still do. I could never understand what made you leave me. You never cared to check on me or find out if I was alive. You asked no one how I was doing. Did I mean nothing to you? You moved on as if there was no relationship between us, you forgot me, and today you are behaving like a friend. I want an answer— why did you ditch me? Why did you never come back?"*

I was shocked and trembling with fear. I desperately looked around for help, anyone to stop this man from harassing me. But there was none. He needed closure, and I didn't have answers that would calm him down.

How could I say I lost interest in him because I was a teenage girl? A married man is still hooked on to his ex from school—I couldn't believe it. I started walking away to avoid his questions and his anger that made no sense to me. I had no answers and explanations for him. Furious, he came running to stand right in front of me and held me by my shoulders, *"You can't run away today. Answer me."*

His high-pitched tone scared me, and I bit my quivering lips to answer him, *"I don't think it would mean anything now since you and I both have moved on with our respective partners and are much settled. It's really not important to have this old discussion that would lead nowhere. I didn't mean to hurt you today, but it's surprising that you are holding grudges against me. It's time you move on."*

"Oh, really! Move on!" He yelled at me.

"The one who moved on easily was you. I never moved on. But you will never understand."

He gave me a fierce look before walking away toward the other end of the parking lot, and I sighed in relief. I saw my friends rushing toward us and that was a bigger relief. There was brief chitchat between him and our friends and I heard him telling them, *"I never want to see this girl again!"*

I didn't know how to respond to this; I was speechless. He was a hurt soul, and I did nothing to relieve him of his pain. I didn't give any satisfactory response to his questions. But I guess he got some relief after his outburst at me. The feelings he was holding for so long finally got an outlet.

It is surprising that certain actions taken at a young age can affect someone for so long. I never thought his wound still hadn't healed, and meeting me was like a fresh blow on an open wound!

7

The Wisdom to Accept a
Heartbreak Comes Later in Life

---

*"Some people come into your life
for a reason, a season, or a
lifetime!"* —*Unknown*

After all these years, to be precise sixteen years, what makes an ex-lover hold a significant spot in your heart? Especially someone who hurt you, broke your heart, cheated on you, and wasn't loyal to you. We have all been there, in this situation where you part ways but continue to cherish the memories with your ex; they continue to be the special someone in your life despite the well-settled life you are already living.

Such is the magic of first love. My first love continues to

101

hold the number one spot in my heart, even though I am pretty much happy with my current partner and our life. There is something about first love that makes it special; it never leaves you. The thoughts and the feelings remind you there is nothing stronger than the memories of the initial relationship.

First love is always unique, the feeling of being loved by someone you totally adore puts you on cloud number 9. However, sometimes, things don't go as smoothly as our dreams; sometimes, situations change, and hence partners also change. Often, one partner tries to cope with the hurt while the other one moves on with a different companion. Such is life, and such are relationships. Forgiving, getting over the hurt, and moving on is what life teaches us.

Many times, we hold the hurt feelings inside; it could be sadness or anger, but one phone call from our ex, and the hurt vanishes. We leave behind the bitter experience, and retrospection helps us heal and understand what happened and why it happened.

There is no more hurt, no more grudges, as we figure out the missing pieces in our relationship and understand why it didn't move ahead. Often, we gain this wisdom late in life, and once we gain it, we regret the time wasted in hating our ex, in crying, and trying to cope with the heartbreak.

There is some positive in everything that doesn't act in our favor. It may not be apparent then, but years later we understand the hidden meaning and goodness in decisions that affected us. After all these years, I have finally understood why as a teenager it was difficult to let my lover leave and to accept my breakup. I spent years crying for my love, craving for a text, a phone call, or a glimpse of my love.

We reconnected years later, not as lovers but as friends and well-wishers. I am grateful because I lost a lover then, but I gained a friend now. We continue to be friends and often talk about the time spent together. Both of us continue to be special for each other but lead our lives separately and with our chosen individuals.

To accept the rejection, the heartbreak, and move on becomes easier when we connect the dots that led to the breakup and every move seems justified. I have no regrets, no pain, and no guilt. I am happy I get to spend time with my ex; whatever little time we spent together is beautiful, and I am thankful we continue to be wonderful friends. Not every relationship has a future, but we can definitely make the journey memorable. Let's accept our heartbreaks, our hurts, and move on in life with a positive approach.

LUST

In between love and loyalty,
comes a little bit of lust...it's in all
of us!

1

A Night or a Nightmare?

It was one of those nights that any woman would dread experiencing. Even the most loving partners sometimes become victims of lust and forget the person they hurt by their wild acts. Such acts often leave a permanent mark on the person's identity and relationship. The hurt often gets healed, but the scars remain.

Our relationship was mature, full of love and life; my partner was too much in love with me, more than I loved him. His cousins were visiting us for a casual party that night and his parents were part of the celebration, too. Some mix-up of alcoholic drinks prepared by one of his cousins made him too high and he started behaving like a total drunkard.

Every now and then, he would come too close to me, touch me inappropriately, or try to kiss me on my lips, forcing me to push him back. A happy get-together turned into an embarrassment for me. I was seeking ways to maintain physical distance from him by making random excuses to go to the kitchen or talking to the other members of the family. Thankfully, his parents noticed the uneasiness and embarrassment he was causing me before everyone and asked me to take him inside, in our bedroom, to settle him down. I was so relieved that they understood and walked him to our room.

The moment I closed the door, he was all over me—hugging, kissing, and trying to undress me. Being my husband, it wasn't something offending, but I tried to calm him down and took him to the bed. He tried to pull me toward him, but I resisted and said, *"I will change and come back."*

He wasn't ready to listen. This time his strength was enough to pull me; I fell on him and he instantaneously flipped to get on top of me.

"Give me five minutes, I will come back... now is not the time... can you wait...can you stop, please no," I begged him to stop, but he wasn't listening. In seconds, my top was flying off the bed and he began kissing me aggressively. It became hard to push him away.

I never felt so uncomfortable lying beneath him, struggling to push him away and get some air. He removed my bra and began sucking and kissing my bare breasts. I could not stand the smell of his mouth that would in between kiss my lips, too. I held his head and tried to push him to the side. To this, he responded by holding back both my wrists with his big muscular arms, leaving me crying in pain.

Before he could go down on me, I yelled at him, *"Is this all I mean to you? Is this all you want from me? This is how much you love me that you want to do this to me?"*

There was an immediate reaction—his grip loosened; he got up and was in tears. My anger and my words shocked him. It was as if someone woke him from a deep sleep. I was so furious that I yelled at him once again, *"I hate you for how you behaved with me tonight."*

With tears rolling over my cheeks, I rushed to the bathroom in the bare minimum I was wearing, and anger took over all my love for him.

I kept crying behind the closed doors. My wrists had the deep marks of his tight grip and my body looked red from rashes caused by his stubble. I looked at myself in the mirror.

A shocked and hurt lady stood in the mirror with hickeys on her neck and shoulder that on a normal night would make me laugh, but tonight I hated him for doing this to me. I washed my face and gathered the courage to get out.

He was still sitting there disappointed but jumped out of bed to move closer to me. I stopped him and signaled him to stay where he was. For a second, he scared me, but I think my harsh words brought the emotional and loving husband back in him.

He peered at me with teary eyes and said, *"I am really sorry. I don't know what happened to me. Please forgive me."*

His apology meant nothing to me. Without looking at him or uttering a word, I picked up my blanket to sleep on the couch. He kept saying sorry, but I asked him to leave me alone. I knew he was sorry. He is not someone who would hurt me; it was the mix of drinks that made him desperate and crazy. Yet, to accept the hurt caused by my loving husband was difficult and unimaginable.

That night was the last in our marriage when he forced himself upon me. He never repeated it and has been very mindful of his drinking since then. Also, he is super cautious of how he behaves when he is a little high. Even though that horrendous night does not disturb or upset me, sometimes he intimidates me when I am not in the mood and he comes home drunk.

2

Lust Takes Over Love

It was the month of December; the holiday season was upon us and parties became an everyday ritual. During one such party at a popular pub, I spotted him drinking with a few buddies. Our eyes met, and the expressions changed from happy to surprised, but overjoyed.

After several glances, I kept looking at him to make a connection. He responded by locking the gaze and signaled me to meet outside. Super excited, I excused myself from the party and headed in the direction of the parking lot. He quietly followed me.

That night, I broke the promise to myself and let lust take over love; two high and emotionally charged ex-lovers looked at each other and without uttering a word, began kissing like crazy lovers. Drunk and high, the animal inside both of us forced us to get in the backseat of my car. We kissed and hurried to remove the layers that covered our beautiful bodies.

Our semi-naked bodies touched and rubbed, the lips locked, and our arms wrapped around each other with fingers running over every inch of the bare backs. Before we knew it, we were thrusting and rocking and making rhythm together. 'Sex in the car' once topped our 'to-do wish list.' But today, it was lust and pure lust.

Irrespective of our wishes to stay away from each other at the party, our hearts pointed otherwise. I had no clue he still held the key to my heart and could affect me emotionally. Little did I know that a glimpse of him had the potential of bringing the golden memories of college romance flashing before my eyes; our romantic relationship was a thing of the past, but much cherished even today. He still looked as attractive as he was five years ago.

We were old lovers-turned-strangers since long distance didn't work for us; it wasn't our thing. The struggle to keep the magic alive in our relationship was like an everyday challenge; heated arguments and explanations took over the nightly romantic conversations we earlier enjoyed. We tried everything but failed. The decision to end the relationship was mutual.

We parted ways to accidentally meet after a gap of five years at this party. It wasn't easy for me to get over him, but the entry of a new partner definitely makes it easier for you to get over your ex.

I was going steady with my partner, but the magic of first love never ceases to amaze you. The innocence of first love and the first kiss is invariably memorable for everyone. Regardless of how old we get and the number of companions we change, we are reminded of how it felt when we first fell in love. And if that special someone is standing right in front of you, the memories of initial lovemaking days come alive.

It was hard to ignore each other's presence at the pub. I tried to be normal, but the regret of letting go the most amazing person I had ever met and the guilt of giving up awfully early in the long distance was hitting me inside.

Already craving his touch, I wished to tell him how I felt after the breakup and how much I missed him. When I made eye contact with him, I did not expect to go too far and make love to my ex-lover. But God, it was heavenly!

We were both high on alcohol and carrying emotional

baggage; we could not wait to hold and kiss each other. The backseat of my car is witness to the passion and heat of our lovemaking. I wanted to clear the air surrounding our failed relationship, but what happened between us was not just unexpected but extraordinary.

Naked and fearless, we couldn't resist each other. His toned body appeared too good to touch and the fragrance of his cologne irresistible. All we saw was a naked partner-in-crime who demanded we leave no chance of once again making love. In these five years, both of us had graduated from the sweet, innocent hit-and-trials of sex to the mature, experienced lovemaking tricks. We grinned as we tried to find our clothes, but there seemed no regrets. Maybe this was our closure. We decided to never meet and never talk about it since our present relationships were at stake.

We couldn't afford to ruin that. But a sense of calmness, accomplishment, and satisfaction prevailed like we finally knocked off each other and took the highly-awaited revenge.

What a night it was! Definitely, one to remember!

3

The 22-year-old Intern

I was 38 then, and she was 22—the new intern in my office. My boring, frustrating bedroom life wanted a breather and some excitement. The charm of the young girls who step into the professional world is pretty noticeable; they want to make their mark and impress everyone with their charisma, if not talents.

Her attempts to flirt with me didn't go unnoticed; I always responded well and would enjoy flirting with her. She would make excuses to come into my cubicle and talk for no reason, giving me hints of taking the flirting to the next level.

I made sure I treaded carefully in this arrangement since the young generation is very unpredictable and I have an excellent reputation at my workplace. I needed to be careful and not tarnish my image because of this fling.

There was no chance I would allow a casual affair to wreck my career, especially if this relationship went haywire, and this woman filed any complaint against me.

We had just begun our casual flirting and meetups after work, getting comfortable with each other. One weekend, she invited me to her late-night party that had many more young girls and boys attending. It was an uneasy feeling sitting with the young crowd, busy smoking and drinking like the sun would not rise tomorrow. It reminded me of my college days when day and night wouldn't matter and we would keep our cigarettes and beers handy.

I approached her and expressed my desire to leave. She asked me if it's possible to stay a little longer and I couldn't say no. Her mischievous smile meant something as she asked me to follow her to another room that was dark and vacant. I followed her blindly, thinking about her next move. She closed the door behind her and started kissing me passionately on my lips.

The horny bull inside me reciprocated her warmth by kissing her back. In minutes, we were in her bed, all naked beneath the sheets, finding it hard to keep the lusty desires under control. Her moans were so irresistible, I couldn't keep my hands off her breasts and my lips kissed every inch of her body. She insisted I get inside her for the climax.

As much as I wanted to bang her, I was reluctant since I had no protection. But she was smart to be prepared with condoms under the pillow. The excitement renewed, and we started with missionary and moved to her favorite 'girl on top' position. She looked experienced with all her moves and positions.

The climax was phenomenal considering I had an orgasm after ages; it was missing from my sex life. My wife had not been so experimental and supportive of my sexual desires and pleasures. But this girl could arouse a man, so he makes love to her; she knew the tricks to get a guy in bed and satisfy him. What a pleasurable experience, especially after the long dry spell in my private life!

There was no stopping after that night. She would send me texts and we would end up having sex in the car, parking lots, restrooms, her place, and sometimes hotels. For me, it was pure lust. Like a hungry lion, I would pounce on her and she was no less. She was a crazy freak who enjoyed pain; she wanted me to be her sadist partner.

I have invariably been open to experimenting in sexual

relationships, hoping to end the boredom of my monotonous life. She wasn't the first girl I was having sex with, but she was definitely extraordinary for her age.

Once she challenged me to tie her up for the role-play of a rapist. It shocked me. I am not a rapist. What made her think I could act like one? Her demand made me uncomfortable, and an inner voice said it might mean and lead somewhere else.

I feared false accusations and allegations in the future; she might actually allege rape later. After much consideration, I refused the role-play of a rapist in bed, pissing her off.

Later, when she was fine and normal, she texted me her next demand, which was a threesome with one of my male friends. Inexperienced in a threesome, this sounded like an excellent opportunity with this bold lady. It took some time to convince my friend, but he agreed and we had an awesome threesome at her place.

The horny bitch later asked me to leave the room and enjoyed another steamy session with my friend. Man, she was something! However, there emerged the need to pull out of this arrangement since her craziness and her demands every day were an enormous distraction causing a dent in my professional and personal life. This casual setup had the potential of destroying my married life, which was dead to some extent, but I cared about my four-year-old son. I couldn't destroy my relationship with my son because of a girl who wanted nothing but sex.

I started ignoring her and stopped replying to her texts. It was a little difficult and awkward in the beginning since she worked under me. I had to sit with her on most days at the workstation and ignore her flirtatious signs, asking me to sleep with her.

We were often face-to-face, but I avoided any eye contact with her. It was clear from my gestures and actions that I was no longer interested in this office affair. It ended with her internship since it was time for her to leave and find an actual job.

What an amazing month full of some top action sex and drama, but truly exciting! I don't regret my extramarital affair with her since I needed to break the monotony of my very predictable life. It was a much-needed break; it was like rain in a drought-hit city. I will never ever meet her again, but yes, I fantasize about making love to her; I miss the flirting and our very casual between-the-sheet sessions.

4

What Is Infidelity?

What is infidelity? I didn't cheat on my girlfriend or date anyone else except her. But I admit, I fantasized about making love to a woman I found attractive at my organization. I was not the only one smitten by her glamor; the entire office wanted to be her friend. It seemed sheer luck as she occupied the desk next to mine since I was her reporting manager.

 That made our meetings and conversations very frequent; our after-work chitchats, messaging, phone calls, and occasional drinks became a norm. There were no expectations of a relationship or having a fling with her, for I was already dating my high school love.

My life was pretty much settled with her, and we were

enjoying our committed relationship, but somehow this new colleague was attracting me in every possible way. I wanted to stay close to her and be with her. I would fantasize about making love to her. In fact, sometimes I have wanted to touch her but refrained from doing so.

One Saturday evening, my girlfriend was staying with me for the night. We were both drunk and our Saturday night erotic movie show at my apartment aroused us both. Wasting no time, we got to our favorite part of love-making—sex. While in the act, I could only imagine my new work partner instead of my girlfriend. I was so high I thought I was kissing and banging my beautiful colleague. I could sense her naked body rubbing against mine. I touched and kissed her boobs and as my strokes intensified, I could hear her soft moans.

My mind seemed out of control; I wanted her. I kept on thrusting and stroking while my girlfriend was enjoying my aggressive side. As I was about to climax, I inadvertently said her name and passed out on my girlfriend.

The next morning was like a painful investigation that ripped apart my imaginations and fantasies as my girlfriend fired multiple rounds of questions that blew my mind. I told her I wasn't cheating on her and that I am a loyal partner, but she had already made up her mind that I was sleeping with someone else. I proved my honesty and loyalty when I told her I was only fantasizing about my colleague and all men do that.

There is nothing wrong with it. But she went crazy and termed it as infidelity! Really? Is it infidelity? To dream about another woman but staying loyal to your partner? I don't understand my lady sometimes. Has she never dreamed of sleeping with someone else other than me? Is there no guy that wants her attention and attracts her more than me? Is that infidelity, too?

In the past, I have fantasized about many women; I have masturbated dreaming about making love to them. Many times, I kiss my girlfriend, but I am dreaming about someone else. This does not mean I am disloyal; she means the world to me. But being a man, my sexual desires and fantasies differ from hers. Not all men talk about or admit to fantasizing about other women when having sex. I did it, and maybe that was my biggest mistake. To make a woman understand a simple theory seems impossible sometimes, let alone defining infidelity in my words.

It took me months to convince her and prove my loyalty,

but what am I going to do if she hears some other name during our intimate moments? It was difficult to win her back, and I am trying to build trust again between us. For me, love is when you remember your commitment to your partner, and infidelity is when you forget that commitment and get carried away by attraction. What do you think?

5

Who Did I Get in the Bed With?

She kept crying in pain but I wouldn't stop, after all, it was our first night together. I had been looking forward to having her in my bed; I had imagined so many ways of caressing her soft body, of having sex with her on our first night. It was my day, our day, and even though I knew she was shy, she was desperately waiting for me to get inside her.

She was crying yet enjoying it; she was both moaning and smiling. I could sense pleasure on her face that gleamed with all the love I was showering on her. I secretly had Viagra to make the sex memorable, and while my strokes must have been painful for her, she seemed equally desperate. She pushed me aside to get on top and took the lead. Her bare breasts were almost swinging on my chest and I grasped them to give them support. She moaned faintly as we continued to make synchronized rhythm.

It surprised me to see her shyness take a backseat as she went all over me, giving me hickeys here and there. I asked her to stop, but she wouldn't—she had become too wild. As much as I was admiring her passionate side, the hickeys on my neck were bothering me since my friends would figure them out and make fun of me.

Despite the dilemma, I let her do whatever she liked just to enjoy the moment and her fiery side. I had not imagined the bold side of her; she was always the shy girl who I could overpower with my physical strength.

She always came across as an innocent girl, submissive to my animal strength. I had imagined myself as the villain who would strip her naked in full light and lick her body inch by inch. She turned out to be a tigress waiting to overpower me with her demands and wouldn't let me stop. To please her in bed was difficult as she wanted more kisses, touching, and foreplay. It seemed to me that my taking Viagra had all the positive impacts on her!

Tired and almost done, I signaled to her that I was about to cum. She smiled and let me ejaculate. Our breathing became heavier as we got off the rhythm. She was all sweaty and insisted we get in the shower together, giving me a sultry smile. Not expecting any more action from her end, I was a bit surprised by her demand. I complied since it would be foolish to say NO to a naked young woman seducing you in the shower! A chance too good to ignore!

I stood behind her to cup her breasts with my hands and squeezed them gently. With water falling on our heads, I found it difficult to open my eyes and watch her, but she seemed aroused once again. The shower noise suppressed her moans, but her actions and expressions suggested she was enjoying my touch.

She turned around and pushed me on the wall to kiss me on my lips. I guess I was waiting for it. The shower prevented me from enjoying the soft touch of her lips, but I continued to satisfy her. Finally, she took a step back; maybe she was tired and done. She came out of the shower, dressed in a silky black nightgown, looking irresistible and attractive. I too got dressed, followed her, and we got cozy in the bed.

Considering her sexual desires and energy, I prepared myself for another steamy session and kept some condoms by the bed. However, she didn't utter a word and slept like a baby, only to wake up straight in the morning and act as if nothing happened between us.

I looked at her, but she couldn't look me in the eye. She was back to her old self; she became the same timid, shy, and submissive girl I met a few months ago. I tried asking her questions about last night and all she did was smile. It was weird to see the tigress get uncomfortable and intimidated by my questions. She walked out of the room, giving me her sweet smile but leaving me confused and baffled.

Did I wake up from a vivid dream? Or am I dreaming now? The dots do not connect, and everything looks like a puzzle. I asked myself—what did she smoke last night? Am I with the right girl? Who did I sleep with?

6

Love and Lust: What Lasts Longer?

I will start by affirming my love for my husband. We have been married for thirteen years and are continuing bright and strong. Like every couple, we have enjoyed the bliss, had fights, and suffered setbacks, but we invariably stood by each other, irrespective of the situation. This is also the reason we trust each other blindly.

Everything was progressing fine that day as we prepared to host my husband's friend, coming from London to stay for two days. I had never met him in person and only heard stories about the wonderful old bachelor days from my husband. This meeting was also a reunion party for a few college buddies who were looking forward to welcoming their dear friend from London.

The taxi stopped right outside our gate, and my husband hurried to welcome him. His excitement was beyond normal. As they hugged each other, I looked at my husband's friend and he looked at me; we greeted each other and made brief eye contact. Something was undoubtedly attractive about him that pulled me toward him, and I noticed his eyes looking for me every few minutes. Even though I had seen his pictures and watched him in old videos, he looked better in-person.

There was an unusual spark between us; his muscular, toned body and his sharp looks mesmerized me. I barely talked and only observed him. After our big lunch, my husband excused himself to attend a short business call, and I grabbed the opportunity to show my husband's friend his room for the two-day stay. While I gave him a tour of the house and his room, he remained a silent spectator, as if admiring my looks and waiting to kiss me. Shy and uncomfortable, I smiled and excused myself to attend to the kids.

The party began early as all the friends started pouring in with their respective partners; he was the only bachelor, still single and hot. He would occasionally come and help me with serving food and drinks and doing other chores. I was more than happy to see him around me, but somewhat also a little scared since my mind and heart were giving varied signals.

After a fantastic evening of singing, dancing, memories, and good old tales, everyone bid goodbye. My happy and high husband was too drunk to help me with the post-party cleanup; he apologized and retired to his room. But his friend stayed back and helped me tidy up the mess despite having a few drinks.

I requested that he sleep since it was a long day for him, but he ignored my suggestion and continued to help me clean up. Finally, we called it a night and switched off the lights to head to our respective rooms.

As I lay in bed, I kept thinking about him, the way he looked at me and helped me in the kitchen. His eyes were magical. Without saying a word, he said a lot. It aroused me, and I felt the need to satisfy my sexual urge. I looked at my husband who was snoring loudly, drained after the booze party that left him happy-high after so long. I got out of bed and quietly knocked on his door. The shirtless hot bachelor opened the door, his muscular body asking me to hug and kiss him. He looked at me, pulled me inside, and locked the door. Without saying a word, we began kissing and making love to each other. In seconds, our clothes flew and landed on the floor; we were naked under the blanket.

His muscular chest was pressing my bare boobs, his boner teased me so hard that it turned me on. We went wild; without uttering a word, we fought over getting on top. He won as he held my arms above me and penetrated deep inside. I moaned with pain and joy as we continued to make love. Suddenly, the fear of getting caught disappeared, and I started enjoying the sensual pleasures.

It was the most magical night I experienced in my lifetime. I got up to grab my clothes, trying to locate them in the room's darkness. He kept his gaze on me as I dressed to go back to my room. His drunk eyes expressed more than the words can justify, but awkwardness prevented me from establishing eye contact with him. I hurried up to leave and gave him a quick glance. He was still in the bed. His gaze drifted from me to the door.

That night, despite the tiredness, I couldn't sleep. There was excitement and sexual contentment, but there was also guilt. I looked at my husband who was still snoring, unaware of his wife's fling with his best friend. My restlessness grew as I imagined his reaction to my infidelity. I was dreading the morning and wasn't confident of how I would face my hubby.

The guilt had sunk in. I had given in to my sexual desires and broken the trust that we as a couple had; I couldn't believe I slept with another man, my husband's friend. But I also couldn't deny the attraction between us the moment we had met.

The next morning, I tried to be normal, along with him who was my partner in crime. He gave me a quick glance to say '*good morning*' in a low tone and avoided staying close to me.

There were no talks, no offers of help, and no coming close to me. Maybe he was regretting his actions, too. It was visible from his behavior and expressions that he didn't want any trouble. He spent most of the time, until his flight, playing with the kids and talking to my husband. In between, he would glance at me to make sure my mood was alright.

When it was time to leave, he hugged my kids, my husband, and then gave me a light, formal hug and whispered 'sorry' in my ears. I was an equal partner in the act, but I couldn't respond since my family was right next to me.

It's been five years since my fling, and my husband knows nothing about it. He still talks to his friend, which means his friend has buried our little secret in his heart, and I am truly thankful to him. Oftentimes, I feel guilty, but I have accepted that I cannot change the past.

There are moments when the guilt pushes me to take the burden of the fling off my chest, but then I remind myself about his friendship with my husband. It's better to forget about the fling. I often reminisce about that night, and I cannot deny that it was lust that brought us together. Yet, that night remains the most special, wild, and unforgettable chapter of my life.

7

The Stranger I Love

I am in love with my sensual dreams, my imaginations, and my power to create love-making stories—all with you and about you! Who are you? A stranger who has hijacked my power to think straight? I am constantly daydreaming about someone I don't know! You are a face with the identity of my lover; you are the one who controls my emotions and someone I like to make love to. I think you exist solely to fulfill my physical and emotional needs.

It started with a faint idea of having a perfect love relationship with someone willing to share the same passion and intensity as mine. With no real partner, the desire to be in a relationship led me to weave unlimited stories about our attraction, love, and lust.

My mind is constantly dreaming about you, it creates visuals of us getting intimate in the most sensual way; my heart skips a beat when I imagine the deep intimacy we share in bed. We do not limit our romance to the bedroom. To up our game, we explore different zones and sensual spots wherever and whenever we like. Am I crazy to imagine our 'between-the-sheet' acts, or is it normal for a girl to fantasize about a stranger she loves?

The touch of your lips as they move on my face in the elevator, trying to hold my lips in your mouth, arouse me enough to stop the elevator midway and indulge in foreplay. Your strength when you lift me in your arms makes me feel safe and guarded; I am aroused by your hands running over my legs and under my skirt in the car's backseat. I hear my own moaning as you lay on top of me in the missionary style, trying to get inside me. Are you someone from my past life? Someone I once dated or married? How can my brain imagine so many details, especially when you are a total stranger?

All I see is a face that looks lovingly at me, who longs for me, who follows me everywhere to protect me. It is unbelievable that a complete stranger in my dreams has made me fall in love with him. I am almost certain that you exist somewhere, and one day I will find you. The magic of your love is such that I don't pay attention to any other men who notice me, for I have my heart set on you.

You are in your true sense a thief who stole my heart and my senses that help in differentiating between truth and imagination. I hate to believe you are my imagination, someone I created for my own reasons, my sexual needs. I gave you the power to become the most important person in my life. Now, look what you have done to me! It seems impossible to get you out of my dream world and accept the reality. I want to keep making love to you and keep you in my arms forever!

I don't know if I hold a chance to meet someone like you in this life, but I would prefer this love story to be mine someday. Are you listening? You better do because you're stuck with me. I trapped you in my brain!

MEMORIES

*Some chapters are best kept secret;
somewhere in our heart they stay
preserved!*

1

My Photo Doesn't Belong to You

As I was packing my stuff, ready to move into my new house, I saw you watching me with despair. You said nothing, yet you expressed a lot with your eyes. I noticed it hurt you, but I also knew what was best for both of us, at least for me. Your actions compelled me to make the firm decision, and I had no reason to change it. Your infidelity, your cheating, and your lies had already caused turmoil in my life. You became the reason for my pain, and even though you changed, it was difficult to trust you again. I was just done with you.

It was you who drove me to my new rented apartment, much smaller than what you had bought for me, but sufficient and affordable for now. You helped me with moving and settling down in the new house, taking care of necessary arrangements to make my transition smooth.

There was a strange silence between us—we were talking, yet we were not. You were trying to make eye contact, and I was trying my best to avoid it. It wasn't because of any guilt; I didn't want your sad face to make me weak and change my decision.

I could understand your pain, but I could also not forget my frustration and anger when you didn't care for me and lied to me to be with someone else. The pain of betrayal hasn't left me. Today, you are loyal to me, but I guess I have moved on.

We sat on the floor as you got busy with utility bills on my laptop. I saw your wallet right beside me and I remembered you keeping my picture in it. I thought about the day when you took my picture from me, placed it in your wallet, and said, "*My wife, my lucky charm must stay close to my heart and inside my wallet.*"

Love was at its peak then. I never thought you would cheat on me and take my affection for granted. It was time to make you realize that your lucky charm was no longer lucky for you and you must learn to live without her.

I quietly grabbed the wallet, making sure you didn't catch me. I took away my picture and kept it in my bag. My picture no longer belonged to you. I wanted you to feel the same emptiness in your heart that I had, every time you opened your wallet. While it was bitter to steal my last piece from you, it was important to move ahead in life, both for you and me. You must have figured out in a day or two about the missing picture from your wallet, and I hope it reminded you I am forever gone from your life.

I still don't understand how I summoned the courage to take the bold step of separation and lead a single life. Today, when I think of that day, I remember your sad face but I also pat my back because I am happy where I am now, and not for once do I regret my decision of parting ways. Sometimes, you need to move on without turning your back.

Yes, memories and moments hold you back, but, remember, time is the biggest healer. Nobody can stop you from being happy and finding your true soul mate. When the time is right, everything falls into place and your decisions take you to your perfect spot and destination.

2

Stalking

How do you figure out you are over someone? How do you know you are no longer interested in knowing anything about them? It is when you stop stalking them and their social media profiles! Simple! Isn't it? Well, not so simple.

The world of social media reminds us of our past by continuously showing us posts related to them and bringing up memories in notifications. It makes the hard process of getting over and moving on in life slow, yet we allow it to hurt us.

I don't understand why I stalk you now and then. It's not like I want to be with you once again, it's not like I love you anymore, yet I stalk you on your social media almost every day. Maybe, I want to check if you have moved on. And what am I supposed to do or perceive if you have moved on? Do I want to watch you suffer or post sad poems and quotes in memory of our once healthy relationship? I don't get what I will learn by checking your posts every day. Despite promising myself to never look back at you, I am inclined to constantly figure out how you are faring socially and professionally. I guess I want to see if you found a new partner already.

Will that make me happy or will that make me stop stalking you? It is still a question. Am I looking for closure? Did we not end it peacefully, with no arguments? Or did we just fall apart because of our constant fights? Whatever! I have discovered positive reasons to move forward in life, and I hope you, too, have figured out ways to stay sorted and sane.

Wait, are you stalking me, too, on my social media? Well, that would be interesting. Are you interested in figuring out who I am dating now? Isn't that too early? If you would still like to check out my current status, I can post my picture with someone to make you super jealous.

But why? Why do I want you to be jealous? We are not together anymore. We are over each other, seeking a stronger relationship with a better person. Then why am I doing things I shouldn't be doing?

I believe to get someone out of your heart causes a lot of pain and seems impossible at first. We get attached to people and learning to live without them is an art. I still find it hard to not talk to you and check my phone pretty often to see if there is any call or any message from you. If I am confident that I don't want us to be together, then what makes me wait for a text from you? It looks like it's time for me to once again check what you are posting on social media. Stalk mode ON!

3

The Weird Feeling that I Enjoy

It is a weird feeling when you have moved on, yet you are stuck on your ex; you love your partner, yet you keep a check on your ex; there are no expectations from your past love, yet you expect something. You wish the best for your lover, yet you are jealous of his or her current flame. It's a bittersweet symphony of life—the sweet heartaches caused by ex-flames are part of memory, even though you have no business with them.

Also, there is no intention of having them back in your life, but you like to keep a tiny flame of false hope alive in your heart. Without this flame, the warmth is insufficient, the excitement is inadequate, and the symphony is non-synchronous.

It seems bizarre to me that someone as dedicated as me would sometimes ignore my family life to finish my chitchat with him; even though I am thankful for my present life, my partner, and family, I still imagine how it would be if we were together! How would we react if we bumped into each other?

What would we talk about if we accidentally sat next to each other on a flight? The heart loves to imagine distinct probabilities that can bring us together again, but the mind is constantly with the present partner and family. Can't the heart and brain sync and root for the same team? Why do they have to confuse us with different dreams and hopes and then present us reality, too?

Some memories never leave you; he is one such memory that is my favorite and never seems to fade. I like to check on him via social media; I like to keep a track of the times he is online. We do not interact, but his being online gives me some kind of hope.

My heart breaks every single day since I receive no message from him, yet I wait for another day and another time when he will be online and ask me about my whereabouts. The false hopes, the heartaches, and the constant chase give me a new kick each day. I guess a little excitement is needed in our day-to-day life to push the monotony aside and keep our hearts young!

We all desire someone related to our past to remind ourselves of the splendid times spent with the wonderful individuals and how fortunate we are to be with our special someone now. Our present lives wouldn't have been possible without the lessons learned from our past relationships.

It would be wrong to term it as cheating or infidelity; these are feelings that stay dormant in our hearts. How can you expect your mind to never speculate about someone you once loved so dearly? How can you stop your mind from fleeing back to the exciting, old times when youth was at its peak and you committed mistakes that you would not want your kids to learn or commit in their lifetimes?

I like to let my mind wander sometimes. It knows its limits and its way back home. Like a parent, I realize when to pull the strings to avoid flying awfully far. We must be free to recreate any scenes from our favorite moments of the past; we must allow ourselves the freedom to think and fantasize about anyone, be it from past or present.

You are not breaking any rules by secretly keeping someone in your heart and wishing the best for them. You know where your loyalty is, so why worry about little heartaches, bittersweet symphonies, and the magic of false hopes and dreams! Let your mind wander and see the excitement it brings to your life!

4

The Hidden Gems of the Past

It's kind of romantic to preserve and protect little gifts from your past relationships. They bring back the memories of the bond that was once strong and special. Those moments that are still alive in our hearts often bring a smile to our faces. Certain little details are a reminder of the propitious life you spent with a truly significant soul.

Accidentally discovering lost gifts and souvenirs, hidden somewhere in an old bag or my closet, is like a treat for the eyes. A dried rose in an old novel seems as fresh as the day they gave it to you, along with a kiss. You hesitate in getting rid of an old book because it was a present to you from your ex. Irrespective of whether you want to read it all over again, you wish to keep it safe on your bookshelf. These precious gifts are like a flashback of the beautiful moments spent with a partner you expected would be yours forever.

Your life had a purpose, and you became special for them only to realize that nothing lasts forever. You hold on to the little treasures not for their value, but for the people who presented them to you.

Regardless of why the relationship ended, it gave you endless happiness, some splendid moments, few lessons, and a companion, even if they didn't stay for too long. These little pieces from the past also make you realize that the fragrance of a fresh flower doesn't last forever; it dies. You were once special to someone and now you are not. They have passed on the baton to someone else.

Some past relationships mean terrible memories, and you wish to erase them from the timeline of life. Associations that do not have a happy ending compel us to get rid of anything that reminds us of our bad choices and decisions. However, if you dig deeper, there were lessons you learned—about trust, promises, never lasting feelings, and of course, people. Trash everything that reminds you of the bitter past—it is the strongest thing you can do in such situations.

Some partners become part of our lives for a reason and for a season. So, instead of crying over a failed relationship, learn to celebrate the experiences and memories we built with them. And if that makes sense, the end of a relationship must not upset us. Instead, it appears like the world has come down crashing on us for we cannot bear the pain of rejection, separation, betrayal, and lost feelings.

Go back into the timeline of your past relationships and check if you have healed from the hurt and pain they caused. Do they still bother you? Do you still hold the same pain? Chances are you have healed now!

Many old relationships do not matter after a certain age. Regardless of how deep the love was, their thoughts and appearances do not bother you. It seems you were never in love with them. Strange, isn't it?

In this transient world, nothing is permanent; forget about love or lovers. So, cherish all that existed in the past, appreciate your present, and be hopeful of a brighter tomorrow! Relinquish the bitter feelings for your ex and be thankful for the love of a considerably better soul that you have.

5

The Misunderstanding

We create memories so that years later they remind us of the beautiful past, spent with someone special. Memories come alive when we glance at old pictures, school scrapbooks, old audios, and videos. We do not always physically possess everything we shared with our lovers and often leave behind certain matters of the heart as we grow old; some memories we also forget with age and time.

While listening to the old tapes that we recorded during college, I recalled the time my relationship with him was at its prime; life appeared perfect, and every plan seemed like it would hold the course we preferred. Our dreams, our aims, and ideas sounded like the perfect way to live life and always seemed like a party in our backyard. Overzealous youngsters often think that way. We hear no complications, have no doubts, or foresee any hindrances.

He and I were perfect together, always making plans of spending our dream life together. But a painful detour drifted us apart, and we never met each other for fifteen years. It was a long time to not meet the person who you loved so dearly. Our perfect party ended unexpectedly, and all our plans got trashed in the backyard.

The notion of a breakup had never crossed my mind; not seeing each other was far from reality for us! Our relationship hit rock bottom and our tender age did not let us find the truth or recover from the damage this caused.

There was no anger, no betrayal, no change of plans. It was just a misunderstanding—a tiny factor that can rip apart your relationship and break you into ten thousand pieces, so you never smile when you reflect on your relationship. All you do is cry and regret your reactions and responses. All these years, I persistently reasoned the silliest part I committed in our relationship and invariably got a slap across my face for doing this to him, to myself.

My biggest mistake, the biggest regret, was to let him go. I never gave him a chance to explain. My impulsive decisions caused me heartbreak; I should have listened to his side of the story!

After almost fifteen years, I saw him at our favorite convenience store today. Everything flashed right before my eyes—our fairy tale dreams, the perfect plans, and the conversational tapes we made to relive youth when we get old. There was a sudden urge to forget everything and give him a tight hug, to say sorry for damaging our once beautiful relationship. I wished to assure him that it was my mistake and not his; I wanted to tell him how much I had missed him and regretted not clearing up any misunderstandings with him. We may not be a couple again, but I wished to apologize for our situation, the unfulfilled dreams, and the unaccomplished desires and for ruining our future like it was solely mine.

I mustered the courage to walk up to him and say sorry for my wrongdoing. How I wished he would look at me and, like old times, understand my pain and how much I have regretted my decisions and letting him go, every single day of my life. I walked to where he was standing in the aisle next to mine, thinking about giving him a bear hug and expressing my feelings, but I didn't see him.

There was no one standing there. Where did he go? I ran to the other aisles to check, but he was nowhere. I looked at the checkout and outside the store, but he was nowhere.

Did I actually see him at the store or was it a hallucination? Did I imagine him standing in the next aisle? I believe it was him. Yes, he was very much there. My eyes couldn't deceive me—I am not that old!

But he disappeared. He left me like I once left him.

6

Can Exes Become Friends?

Many people say ex-lovers cannot become friends because they have a past that connects them and brings along memories that might come in between the friendship. Well, it could be true. I connected with my ex after almost nineteen years, and it brought back fresh emotions and feelings. I couldn't believe we stayed out of touch for nineteen long years. Thanks to social media, I check his profile now and then to learn his whereabouts and be sure he is alive somewhere in this world.

There is something about love relationships; they never let you forget the person no matter what led to your breakup. My relationship with him wasn't the long-lasting one, but it was deep for someone as emotional as me. I fell in love and continued to love him even after he dumped me.

It is strange how I survived the heartbreak, letting no one

see my tears or sense my sorrow. Today, I look back and the memories of our little dates, chitchats, and his touch are still fresh. Those streets, the restaurants where we met, and all the places we visited together remind me of him. But I learned to live with that sense of void in my heart. Of course, I moved on, but he remained forever in my heart. I got into another relationship but never forgot him; I married but never stopped checking his profile on social media.

Today, nineteen years later, he still occupies a teeny tiny place in my heart and makes me cry when I think of why we couldn't be together. I am very much settled and happy in my marriage, but I still crave for him. I still think he wronged me and I shouldn't have loved him so much. It is unbelievable how I came this far without him. There was always an urge to reconnect, but I guess healing of the heart was essential before his re-entry into my life.

In all these years, he never cared to ask if I existed, especially after how he ditched me. Today, he has so many questions for me. I know he is pretty much happy and settled and so am I, but this reconnection has caused a fresh current flowing throughout my body. There is some excitement and reminiscing of events and memories but obviously no hope. There is just a yearning to be his friend now, someone he can trust and open up to discuss his goals, aspirations, desires, and fears. I wish he thinks of me as a friend he can trust and talk about anything and everything, and I want him to be my friend, too.

He could become someone I turn to whenever I want to share or discuss anything, big or small. Is there a possibility of such a friendship between us? Or will our past resurface every time we sit down to talk? My friends suggest I stay away from him and not get all dreamy about this new connection, but I guess we may become friends and be normal with each other.

We have grown old now, pretty mature to handle the emotional baggage from the past, and our family responsibilities will always be our priority. So, it is unlikely that such a friendship will affect me negatively, especially if someday he again cuts me off from his life.

It's like I want to read him once again. I want to ask him questions about his life and his career. I want to understand what has changed and if he still carries the same habits. It feels like I never got to know him much when we were dating, but I distinctly remember some moments, his laughter the most. There is a desire to meet him and see if he still carries the same infectious smile and makes everyone laugh out loud with his jokes.

I am not pinning my hopes on anything or asking him for any favors. There is a hope that someday we can sit and debate the dating days, joke, laugh, and be the good friends who stick together. We cannot erase our past, but we can certainly improve our present. But can former lovers become friends? From lovers to friends is a significant challenge, but I will accept it. I am waiting for him to start the conversation anew for me to explore the unfamiliar side of him. Fingers crossed!

7

Holding on to the Mental Images from the Past

It is strange how we carry a mental image of our loved ones in our mind and like to always imagine them in the same shape and age! We forget that a person grows and will reflect signs of aging, too. Think about childhood lovers who part ways but continue to keep each other in their hearts and minds, only to discover a deformed version of the one they loved dearly. Or maybe you dumped someone based on how they looked and behaved, and years later they are in their best form and you regret the decision you took in the past.

The decision to date someone can change based on not just looks but also behavior and maturity. Young couples often part ways because of the difference in maturity levels as they grow; teenage lovers find new love because the pimples they initially admired on their lover no longer appear sensual; a girl who ignored the proposal of a young but jobless guy suddenly realizes his true potential when he builds his business empire. Relationships often change with time, and there is nothing wrong with it. Better to be with your perfect partner than with the wrong one.

When I reflect on my past relationships, I think about all the amazing partners I have dated; some I dumped as I matured and understood more about how practicality plays an important role when you decide to settle down. I am sorry for hurting those who loved me so dearly. I wish I could explain to them why and how they didn't fit well in my life pattern and why a future with them didn't seem workable.

There wasn't anything wrong with them; they just didn't fit well in my growth pattern. If they ever question my decision, I will happily explain to them why I drifted away, but that would require an open mind and heart because the truth often hurts.

I believe time teaches you a lot and also answers many questions for you. As we grow and look back on our past relationships, we realize how well we moved on. We also learn why certain relationships didn't work out. This is one big factor in the healing process and also helps you get rid of any hurt or grudges. We all have suffered heartbreaks and have hurt others, too. But we should always remember the good times our previous partners brought to our lives. Happiness and happy times are worth remembering instead of the pain.

Life is a journey where you continue to move on despite hurts, betrayals, love, or hate. The important part is to continue to learn, grow, acknowledge, and appreciate since it eases the recovery process and takes you in the right direction. I have broken hearts, faced cheating, and suffered heartbreak, too, but today, I hold no grudges and no regrets. My present partner is more than perfect and a blessing, but I am also thankful for all the splendid memories my exes created with me. I hope my thoughts always bring a smile to their faces. Gratitude!

8

The Little Girl with The Umbrella

My morning walk had just started when the clouds turned black. The forecast did not predict rain in the morning hours, but it began shortly while I was at some distance from home. Unprepared for the wet walk, I wondered where I should run for shelter.

While I rubbed my eyes to wipe off some water, I noticed a couple with a little girl taking out some stuff from the trunk of their big blue SUV. The reason the cute little girl caught my eye was familiarity. She resembled someone I knew dearly, someone from my college days I loved with all my heart. I had a huge crush on her, but she was dating some other lucky guy then. I still loved her and dreamed about her. It was only after the busy work schedule tied me to other responsibilities that I could move past her. The flashback of the old days in the pouring rain made the past appear fascinating.

I stopped for a second to glance at this little girl who had the uncanny resemblance to her—my crush in college. Is it really possible for the little girl to be her child? As I drenched myself in rain, my gaze was stuck on her. I tried to look at her parents to confirm if she indeed was the child of my crush. It was tough to get a glimpse of them, and it was not okay to keep peering at someone unknown. The impatient me walked a little closer to them; the little girl holding her 'Frozen' umbrella looked at me and was surprised to see me all drenched in water.

Amidst slight noises and falling rain, they dragged out the luggage from the trunk. As they straightened their backs and pulled the upper half of their bodies out of the trunk, their faces remained covered with the enormous bag they were holding together.

It felt wrong to stay there, trying to figure out who they are. I did not want them to assume I was trespassing or intruding by staying too close to their property. The little girl was already looking at me with suspicion. I walked past them, and my heart told me to turn around for the last try if I could see the family.

The moment I turned around, I couldn't believe who I saw. I never expected them to be a couple. How was it possible? And what were they doing in my neighborhood? Had they recently moved here or were they visiting someone? So many questions and not one answer.

I quickly turned around to hide my face and kept walking. I looked at the street name to remember where exactly I spotted them. The little girl said something to her parents, but before they acted, I walked swiftly to turn left on a different street. She had something in her eyes that spoke a lot to me. I wanted to talk to her and ask her if she knew me. Is it possible her parents told her about me and my love story, how I had a huge crush on her mom, or why they swiped me out of their life? Or maybe she found my pictures in an old college album and recognized me?

I reached my home and quickly changed into clean, dry clothes. The rain had made me completely wet. While I towel-dried my hair, my lost mind was thinking about our past and the little girl. The mystery surrounding this family made me hurry and grab the car keys to find out what was happening. I drove around the neighborhood and parked the car on their street, but they were nowhere to be seen.

The car was missing, too. I regretted going home. If I had stayed, I would have known their story and reconnected with them. After all, we were once friends. So, what if we did not stay in touch? It was time for reconciliation after the misunderstandings that ended our friendship!

Nostalgia hit me so hard. I couldn't stop thinking about good old college days, about love, dreams, planning, and the final blow that severed our relationship. Jealousy, insecurity, and a desire to be with my lady love led this guy, now her husband, to accuse me of cheating, possessiveness, and whatnot. I was not what he accused me of; I was someone who cared and loved both of them.

The saddest part was that she believed him and distanced herself from me. Their betrayal broke me; I stopped going to college and stopped meeting people. No one asked me why. It ached to be hurt by someone so close, someone I truly loved.

Today, looking at them, I realized they stayed together to marry and now have a daughter. I am now convinced they were always meant to be together. Their love was genuine, and they stood by each other to take their relationship to the next level.

I am unsure if it is their house or if they are visiting someone because I don't see the car anymore. If they are living here, would it make sense to meet them? Would I someday bump into them? I don't know, but I felt their daughter definitely knew me. It would be wonderful if we settled the differences, the misunderstandings, and reconnected for old times' sake!

GRAY MATTER

Perspective is often key to
happiness!—Unknown

1

The Narcissist in My House

The therapist confirmed he is a narcissist—someone who sees himself above everyone else, needs constant praise and attention, and exploits everyone (especially me) without guilt or shame. The last few years have been challenging since figuring out the behavior of this guy I call my husband was complex.

He is definitely not the one I married since he is indifferent to my likes and dislikes. Why he never bothers to answer me when I ask him a question, why he has no love for me, why he is completely different with friends and family, and the opposite with me? Before losing my mind completely, I pushed myself to see a therapist and understand what's wrong with him or if something is wrong with me.

My therapist, who also is my friend, confirmed that my so-called husband is suffering from a narcissistic personality disorder. While this was a relief because it confirmed that I am not the one who is insane, it was also worrisome news since people with this kind of mental disorder rarely change. The best solution offered by my friend was a divorce. The second, and challenging solution, was to accept, ignore, and have zero expectations from him. Neither of these sounded workable and satisfactory because all I was concerned about was my girls and their future.

I am someone who loves to laugh and make other people merry. I am considered a comedian by my family and friends. He is someone who once possessed the sense of humor that matched mine but has lost it somewhere. Our long-distance relationship lasted for about 8 years before we tied the knot. To love someone so much that you give up your dreams and aspirations and make sacrifices only to end up being mentally tortured every day makes me regret this big decision I took fourteen years ago.

It is hard for anyone to accept that a smiling, light-hearted person like me has such a tragic married life. It is also hard for my family to believe that my husband, who is responsible, warm, and welcoming, could be a narcissist. I am insulted and mentally tortured by my narcissistic husband, often bullied for my lifestyle, my looks, and what I do in a day. It is my same character and lifestyle that once was super-appealing to him. Today, he criticizes me for every little thing he once loved about me.

I don't feel a thing for him, but I realize my girls need their Dad. He absolutely adores them, loves them, takes good care of them; he is the perfect father for them. The prospect of a divorce looks appealing to me but is not financially workable for someone who spent fourteen years of marriage trying to become the perfect mother and wife, and not a career woman.

For the world you are someone, and for someone, you are nothing! This holds true for both of us since I am the happiest in his absence and vice versa. We live in the same house, but do not exchange gestures or words. I am mostly nonexistent for him. If I ask questions, he ignores them. When I call out his name, he never responds. I cook food that he often dumps.

But when there is an outsider in our home, he changes completely to become the sweetest person on earth. His silence, more than anything else, is super annoying and often targeted specifically at me.

I am not seeking suggestions to improve my life living under the same roof as him. I understand I need to stay away from him for my own mental peace and sanity, but some decisions are difficult, especially when you know of the painful consequences.

Some people may criticize me for living with a dead, narcissistic soul, but sometimes you know more than what outsiders understand. I have to watch out for my girls, and I am constantly working toward finding a better solution for a decent life for us.

I am one of many women who knew the person they are marrying but were unfamiliar with their personality disorder. It is important to realize that anyone can be a narcissist—a father, mother, husband, wife, son, or even a daughter. You could be living with a narcissist, wondering about their weird behavior.

Seek help if you think your partner has done nothing but shame you, demoralize you, and tried to bully you. Believe me, this kind of torture is way worse than physical torture. I have found solace in friends and my therapist and feel better each time they trust and support me. They boost my confidence. Soon, I will be free from the world of narcissism that exists in my house. Until then, I am keeping my hopes alive with a smile on my face.

2

Why Do You Exist Only in Dreams?

Someday, you will walk out of my dreams and into my life, and I will hold you tight to never let you slip out of my arms. Someday, I will express the strong desire I possess to be in your arms, kissed by you, and to sleep with you. Isn't it amazing that the human brain can create its own imaginative person based on the compatibility criteria?

We can create endless, imaginative stories with this dream person and be part of diverse situations with them —both romantic and unromantic. We can mold any case to be in our favor or convert a serious situation into a lively, romantic scene. When there is no genuine lover in the heart, the human brain can create and love someone that exists purely in dreams!

I have the mental image of this special person who is a replica of the real-life partner I have consistently desired. He is handsome, tall, and a hopeless romantic who loves me more than anyone else. We share similar madness for each other, along with dreams and visions for a better future together.

The sense of security and belongingness that someone's love brings along makes you stable and a better person. Although this character reigning over my head is not real, my dreams make me feel wanted and loved. His words and touch appear real and make me want to know him more. The love we shower on each other is perfect for keeping the relationship strong.

Sometimes, I can't believe the amount of trust and loyalty we have between us. Such perfection can exist solely in dreams since there are no villains, no tight situations, no worries, and no lies. There is only an abundance of love between lovers.

It was in my dreams that you were born. I gave you a face and a magnificent physique that I would love and I changed my character, too, for better compatibility. Love, at first sight, is what you experienced when you saw me outside my workplace and chased me like crazy. You followed me everywhere for months and watched me silently to learn more about me. It was a snowy December night when you approached me outside a coffee shop and asked me out. I don't know what was so special about you, but you attracted me and we connected instantly.

I have many stories about us running in my head; some make sense and some do not. I guess in love, the dots that connect do not always appear logical. The emotional side of you makes me feel loved and extra special. This is all that matters.

Love can do so much to you without you even realizing it. I am always smiling and talking to myself. I guess the entire world is watching me because I am the most beautiful creature created by God and you are somewhere hiding but looking at me. You are a successful, smart, and outgoing man; I am pretty but shy! I am admired by so many, but I set my gaze on you.

In my dreams, I have carved so many stories of you proposing to me, dating, and wedding that I am pretty sure you exist somewhere and I must look for you. One glimpse and I can recognize you even from a distance; I hear your voice, remember your face, and I am sure I know you inside out.

It's disappointing that such a person exists solely in my dreams, and not in the actual world. Can a higher power turn my dreams into reality or pull you out of my dreams and make you an actual person? I wish I could find my soul mate who is an imitation of my dream man, and that will also end my constant switch to the imaginative world to meet my perfect partner.

Someday, I hope you walk out of my imaginative world and stand at the front door with flowers in your hands, asking me to marry you! I wish that is not a dream!

3

No Match Yet the Perfect Match

We were certainly a mismatch for each other, at least for me we were poles apart. He was much taller, talented, and professionally a go-getter. The owner of several companies, he liked to play guitar and piano as a hobby, and was an excellent singer and a fantastic, confident speaker.

He was an amalgamation of talent and knowledge in the human body, a young achiever, and a role model for youngsters. Unlike him, I was an ordinary, but a hardworking employee of a multinational company, who had recently started her career and couldn't match his experience level. As for talents, the only one I possessed was my love for non-stop talking. I could beat anyone in a chitchat competition!

Despite the vast gap between our reputations, talents,

knowledge, and professions, he liked me and pursued me with all his heart. It sounds like a movie plot, but remember, our real-life stories are the inspiration behind romantic movies. This is my story of how a rich guy falls in love with an ordinary girl next door.

At my first meeting with him, I was the one talking more, for two reasons—I was nervous, and I sensed he would reject me. Why would such a tall, handsome, and multi-faceted, super talented person choose me as his life partner?

I lacked the skills that would match his or even complement his lifestyle. I tried to dig deep, yet found nothing he found appealing about me. Maybe in love, there are no logical reasons involved. He had fallen in love with me much before I met him in person, and I was completely unaware of this secret. The revelation happened much later, and everything made sense to me.

He tried to make it appear an arranged meetup by approaching me through a matrimonial website and taking it forward by setting up a casual meeting. The truth is that he already knew much about me before arranging this setup. He was already in love with me and wanted me to love him, too, before taking this relationship forward.

After four meetings, I realized I loved him and wanted to marry him, but it was hard to accept the wide difference in our financial and professional status. I wanted to confess my love, but he seemed way beyond my league. Despite never trying to show off any of his high-class practices, it seemed like a 'no match' to me! I started backing off by ignoring his calls and texts for the fear of falling too seriously in love and having a heartbreak later.

Three days of missed calls and semi-ignored texts passed. It felt terrible to ignore someone like him—a true gem. Some choices are hard, but they make you strong and prepare you for a better future.

The doorbell rang while I was cooking pasta in my kitchen for my roommate and me. I heard someone talking to my roomie, and it sounded like him. Yes, it was him asking my friend about me.

Apparently, they knew each other since he had asked for her help in getting my phone number. She called out my name, smiled, and left. A little surprised and embarrassed in my half-worn clothes, I asked him to give me five minutes to change my clothes. He stood outside, waiting for me to call him in. My heart was beating faster than any Olympian's heart as I looked at him.

"Come in. I was cooking pasta, would you like some?"

"Of course, anything!"

He followed me to the kitchen where my flatmate and he exchanged smiles and she left with her food to give us some privacy. He asked me, *"What's going on? No calls, no texts, no replies. Is everything okay?"* I had nothing to say. He stared at me and asked me to look him in the eye. *"You love me. Don't you?"* I tried to avert his gaze without saying a word. He took the plate from my hands to keep it on the kitchen counter and looked into my eyes, *"I know you love me. What's holding you back? Why are you avoiding me?"*

I had tears in my eyes. I hugged him and said, *"I cannot explain to you why this will never work out between us. There is a vast difference between our professional and financial status. You realize where you stand and where I stand; I don't fall in the same line as you. There are many more things...it might become difficult later."*

"Really? We love each other, isn't that the most important and beautiful part of our relationship? If there is no love, your success or my growth would never matter. Just be with me. I know you love me. We are the perfect match,

made in heaven." Then he smiled.

It was the tightest hug I had ever given to anyone. It also led us to our first-ever kiss. I was so relieved after pouring my heart out as I had nothing in my heart now; the truth shared with him made me feel so much better. We remained in each other's arms for the next five minutes until we heard my roomie coming into the kitchen.

He made a few calls while I got ready to step out with him. He drove me to his place where his parents were waiting for us. I was pleasantly surprised with everyone's warm welcome and familiarity with my name and our relationship. It was his sister who revealed to me at the dinner table how he had fallen in love with me at a party and stalked me to approach through the matrimonial app. The revelation helped me join the dots and now everything, his every move made more sense to me. I wasn't angry or upset; I was happy he was in love with me!

We married in a few months and our relationship has been rock solid since then. That day is etched in my memory because it changed me; all the feelings and emotions poured out of our hearts in a single shot. I still consider him way superior, even though I am the head of one of his companies that generates maximum profits.

He never lets such thoughts come in between our relationship and treats me as an equal. I love the fact that he is still the same lover boy who likes to play guitar and sing for me. Nothing has changed except for his salt and pepper look and a tiny munchkin who takes most of our time.

4

From Fantasies to Reality

It is common for people to bash their partners behind their back. When women meet, their favorite topic of discussion is how and why their partners don't live up to their expectations. Men, on the other hand, enjoy discussions like sports, politics, their careers, and other women.

Women often discuss with friends the shortcomings in their relationships or what they thought their partners would be vs what they have become after the wedding. Why is it that despite all the complaints, regrets, and unfulfilled desires, women like to stick to their partners?

They never give up on them and remain hooked to the idea of having a perfect relationship with them someday. Of course, there are exceptions, but most women bad mouth their husbands but stand strong for them if someone else utters a word against them.

My friends and I joke about our husbands being our biggest mistakes; we discuss our dating days and laugh out loud at the decisions we made to make our lives what they are today. Often, we bash the first friend to marry for not warning us of the consequences of wedlock. We bash the first one to have kids for never sharing with us how difficult it is to raise kids together with someone we no longer find romantic. There is always a reason to criticize our significant other.

Blinded by the dreams of a romantic relationship, we made decisions thinking life will forever be a bed of roses on a beach with no daily chores and no fights, just love, kisses, and sex. It was foolish of us to believe that a dreamworld like our imagination exists. The dreams shattered slowly and gradually, yet the hopes remained. We keep dreaming about the life we imagined for ourselves, but the present keeps knocking on the door until we accept reality.

So, what have we become? We fight, but we don't mend; we are used to each other's tantrums, dislikes, and the whole idea of how the opposite sex is consistently wrong, but we continue to sail in the same boat, year after year. I don't know if my earlier idea of a perfect relationship was a dream or my future hope of having a perfect life is a dream. When dreams shatter, you feel the pain and you regret not listening to the advice of elders. The fantasy realm depicted in movies and novels must be trashed, and everyone must learn that a perfect relationship cannot exist without compromises, adjustments, and the mute button.

Rowing a boat alone vs rowing it with a partner makes a lot of difference. The fear of being alone is what keeps us all together with our partners; some change mates while others learn from their mistakes, but in the end, we all prefer to be with a companion who brightens our lives by their presence.

Everyone wants to open their eyes and see the person they chose as their life partner beside them, and the entire family together. We hate to see shattered lives, and that's what keeps us moving. We get busier and busier and slowly romance slips out and responsibilities take over.

Amidst all this, sometimes we lose ourselves. When we feel lost, we look for a new partner who notices us just like our current partner noticed us long ago. Sadly, the same cycle will repeat even if we find new partners. To love and be loved is not merely a desire, but a necessity in any relationship.

Therefore, everyone must acknowledge the needs of their partner, be it spending more time together, more conversations, romance, or date nights. We all possess the power to move forward in any aspect of life we find interesting. With little tweaks in our habits and behaviors, we can sail the boat together with our partner, even in rough tides.

5

The First and The Last Love Letter

It was after school that he approached me while I was leaving for home. He handed me the letter and left immediately, maybe to avoid any glances from his friends. I didn't know what it was about since it was a regular notebook sheet, neatly folded in two. I knew the boy, and his fondness for me, but I had nothing for him, no feelings, and no friendship.

As I turned around, my friend quickly grabbed the letter from me, running around the classroom, giggling all the way. She insisted on reading it aloud to everyone. All my friends put their bags back on the bench, eagerly waiting to listen to the golden words written on those two pages. While I do not remember the content of the letter, I remember all of us laughing and making fun of me and the boy's feelings.

We were young, grade 12 students, unaware of how difficult it is to express your love through a letter and gather the courage to give it, too, knowing the rejection beforehand. Twenty years later, I do not remember if he had written 'I love you' in that love letter, but I remember his courage, his persuasion, and determination in chasing me even after multiple rejections.

And yes, that was the only love letter I ever received before the internet stormed our world with emails and texts, dethroning our pen and paper era. I would have preserved the letter, but sadly, it was from someone I didn't love and went straight to the trash bin.

In the world of Tinder and social media, why am I worried about that lost page I trashed without thinking twice? Handwritten notes and letters have always touched and fascinated me. We don't do it anymore.

Texts and emails have completely taken over us; love happens over messenger apps and social media. I never received love letters or notes from anyone, only text messages that lack the personal touch; handwritten notes add to the content. I didn't realize the importance of a handwritten love letter back in school and made fun of the poor guy who did nothing but love me.

He was not the smart and dashing kind of guy, but an average, simple, not so attractive boy. He was in the same grade but a different classroom, close enough to watch me, but I am not sure when and how he started following me. I would often see him in my neighborhood, sometimes alone, sometimes with friends. I never doubted his actual intention behind roaming the streets that surrounded my house.

Despite all his efforts, I could develop no feelings for him and had no emotions, no pity, no friendship, nothing. It wasn't like I was a beautiful girl back then. I was an average-looking student with big grandma spectacles and an awful dressing sense, but still a popular girl because of my good grades. I didn't have many admirers; he was the rare one who came forward and the other one was my boyfriend—a senior from my school, studying in a university.

Years later, when I started working, I received a message from him on Facebook that said, "So, I finally found you." Again, I remember nothing in that long paragraph he wrote to me, but it was surprising to see him still following me. I had not seen or heard from him after school; he was like a closed chapter since the beginning for me, but I guess he never stopped chasing me.

He knew where exactly I studied and where I worked. Now it seemed like stalking, but nothing scary. I didn't reply to him; his words didn't change my feelings. I was still the same and nothing had changed.

Today, when I think about all the love and crushes of my younger age, I think about him and I want to ask if I hurt him by not replying to him and ignoring him. He was like the silent lover who kept track of his muse with no intention of troubling her.

For him, love was just loving someone with no expectations, without worrying about the outcome of his one-sided love. I have no clue if he found love in someone else, if he married, has children, or is still single. His partner would definitely be the lucky one since he would love her deeply and stay committed.

I have no regrets in not accepting his love; I still do not feel any inclination toward him. Love is like that, you don't plan to love someone, it just happens. Sadly, I couldn't love him back; I didn't respect his feelings back in school, but I am sure he must be over them now. He must have moved on and must be happy with his family somewhere.

I hope he realizes this someday and understands that I respect his feelings now; I understand how he felt then and I wish him well. To everyone, just be happy someone loves you. It's difficult to find true love in the fast-moving world, dominated by the internet.

6

Fool's Paradise

After all the hurts, lies, and betrayals, you keep coming back to me, and I accept you as if you did nothing wrong. I take you in with open arms and give you my unconditional love. Why I let a cheater and a liar keep his place intact in my heart, I don't know. Each time I let you in, you leave me with no explanation; you hurt me for no reason, and you repeat your mistakes each time. I don't understand what makes you turn back to me and leave me again in no time.

'Not again,' I tell myself and close the doors of my heart for you, the selfish one. I make promises to myself to never fall for you again, only to break them when I see your loving smile and sweet gestures. The moment you say, '*I love you,*' I forget the hurt, the pain, and inch closer to the fool's paradise.

Why is it super difficult to maintain distance from you and tell myself 'absolutely not again'? What makes you come back to me? The moment I decide to move on and seek love somewhere else, I see you and my heart skips a beat. It's hard to not wait for you; it's hard to not think of you. I don't know whether you will return to fool me one more time, or if this was the last time that I would meet you, but I am confident you dream about me and you realize what you do to me each time you leave me. What's not clear to me is why you retrace your steps when I have no permanent place in your heart?

This time, I am determined to not fall into your trap, I will not let you deceive me or play with my feelings. I plan to be strong to tell you to your face that I don't wish to meet you and that my life is healthier without you.

Stop considering me like a highway rest area where you take a mini-break and leave in no time. I am certain I can kick you out of my heart to never fall for you. I am determined to find the love, honest love of someone who will love me with all purity and not dump me as you do. Let me set the stage to show you a different me, the bolder and stronger me.

Don't be surprised by my makeover. I will be forever thankful to you for this transformation. I am sure you will think twice before returning to me next time.

As I practice the strong words that I want to fire at you, I find you standing right outside my door, with the same loving smile that makes my heart skip a beat. Oh! You have my favorite flowers, too. I open the door and welcome you in, forgetting the pain and hurt already. I overlook what I decided, what I needed to express, and I am overjoyed to have you once again. In your arms, I feel the warmth as it comforts me in the cold weather.

Your hugs and kisses make me realize how much I missed them and you! I guess I want more of them. I know I love you; how can I stop loving you? How can I be rude to you? It's just not possible! And here I am, already in the fool's paradise, trying to believe you will not leave, you will not hurt me! I hope I am right just once!

7

Heart: Forever Young and Alive

We all grow up and turn into mature adults; we learn to live with hurts, memories, pain, and sometimes adjustments, too. We accept the decisions that changed our lives and were once right for us. Some twists and turns, compromises, and beliefs change the paths we had initially chosen, but we accept them, too, because we are no longer young to be adventurous and we seek stability.

But what about the heart? It changes, too, with age and maturity, but deep down, it has a desire to revert to the original self, pleading for more passion, intimacy, and romance. No matter how hard I try, I find it difficult to let my heart settle in a mediocre state. I keep turning back the pages to reflect on my past, my dreams, and the imaginative world I built for myself.

With a desire to explore ways of pleasing my heart, I wish

to be the sixteen-year-old seeking ways of finding love, falling in love, having an intimate relationship, and going beyond these words to go crazy in romance.

Sometimes, I regret not doing what I should have done in my younger years, exploring what I did not explore then; I want to be my old, wild self again. I wish to turn back time and enjoy the same excitement, pain, and delusions that love brings your way. The dating phase, the kisses, midnight chats, sneaking out to make out in the car, the naughty and dirty talks—everything we do in love feels right at that age. All the adventurous acts I missed during a young age are what I crave for now. There is a desire to once again go crazy in love, to be that stupid lover who sees nothing beyond his dreams and desires, and who shall happily go an extra mile to win his love.

I believe everything around us is temporary and that only the love in your heart will last forever. Yes, it is true. No matter how many partners you change in your lifetime, a soft corner for each of them exists in your heart. So, what if the relationships ended prematurely? The level of excitement, the passion you once shared with your respective partners, the dreams and beliefs, brought the happiness you cannot deny! Each relationship brought out a different side of you, gave you a unique experience with unforgettable memories, promises, and outlook.

Don't you wish to experience the same newness and the same joy at this age that you once enjoyed in a fresh relationship? The sleepless nights, romantic texts, the desire to meet again, to sleep in somebody's arms, and the dating days make me nostalgic and I crave similar experiences.

I am not young anymore, not in the age to experience a French kiss for the first time, but I wish to relive the initial dating days when relationships were romantic, dreams appeared very close, tears were precious, and for a smile, we could die! There was love, emotions, and romance! I wish I could add the elements of dating to my age-old relationship and experience the joys of the many 'firsts' to keep us forever young and alive!

8

Make Peace with My Inner Self

A young couple sitting right ahead of me in this beautiful patio restaurant, holding hands, expressing love by sweet gestures, seemed carefree and lost in themselves. The visiting server interrupted their romance again and again, but they remained calm and composed. I told myself that *'they must be newly married or must have recently started dating.'*

But when the anniversary cake arrived, the number '10' candle surprised me. This couple was celebrating their 10th anniversary. Really? Does love last that long? Do you still enjoy the warmth of your partner's hand, and of being lost in them so much that you don't realize your surroundings? Really? I was not only surprised but also jealous of not getting the same love.

Why are some couples fortunate in love relationships and

some unhappy? I have been married for ten years and I don't remember the last time my husband held my hand. I do recall the dating days when we couldn't keep our hands off each other. Today, we struggle for each other's touch. I am jealous of all the couples who are still crazy in love, or rather who express their love easily.

I wouldn't claim I am unhappy, but there is an atmosphere that seems ordinary; our relationship lacks love, romance, and sex that are vital for its sustainability. There is respect and fondness which are pretty important in any relationship, but I feel my desires go unnoticed and unfulfilled. Oftentimes, there is an urge to step away and indulge in pleasurable stuff—be it dating, flirting, or even one-night stands. That does not mean I want to cheat on my partner; it's not always about being the loyal spouse in a marriage.

Sometimes life poses challenges and situations that require you to think about your mental state and find happiness outside of your comfort zone. One needs to find a way to achieve what they truly want. If that means cheating, then let's call it so.

I notice men who like to flirt with me and enjoy my company, but I hold myself back for the fear of getting too far with them, ruining my current relationship. What it means to be in wedlock and carry out responsibilities differs considerably from being in a casual relationship that lasts only till the thrill of the chasing game gets boring.

Mine is not a casual relationship; I am married to the person I chose for myself. We dated for a while before taking our vows. To be honest, I dated many men before settling down with my husband; I realized he is the best for a stable married life than anyone else I had dated so far. So here I am, in this relationship that exhibits understanding, respect, attachment, love, but no romance and no physical attraction.

There is care, there is a fear of losing, there are celebrations and gifts, but sensuality, touch, and fun are the elements constantly missing.

Am I too old to seek some attention and romance? No, I am not. I enjoy flirting and romantic conversations, but I will admit such conversations make me uncomfortable when someone goes too far and I fall short of words. I am not certain if I possess the art of flirting back or an easy flow of words to keep the conversation flirty. It seems against my morals, or probably I fear getting caught.

My conscience doesn't let me go beyond a certain point where my ideals and morals clash with my dreams and desires; it doesn't let anyone else come close to me; it doesn't let anyone else touch me. For some women, it is easy to have fun whenever they can, with whoever they want, but for me, it is hard.

It seems unfair that the entire world can have fun, even outside their relationship, but I am reluctant in doing the same. I prefer creating my love stories in my head and I am happy with the re-creations now and then. My imaginations are like the hip-hop playlists that make you dance on the beats and add rhythm to the monotonous life I am living.

I want to hold you tight, just like you would do during our initial dating years; I wish to look into your eyes and say 'I love you'; let's make excuses to touch each other as we did earlier. There are many relationship goals to achieve and less time. Growing old isn't fun, and I guess by the time we realize what we are missing, it will be too late.

I have always dreamed of a perfect romantic relationship, but I failed miserably. I think we are just too busy doing our duties, raising kids, having locked ourselves in the closet. Maybe my dreams do not align well with my partner's goals; I guess this is how my relationship would be. I must make peace with my inner self.

ACKNOWLEDGMENT

There are so many people who cross your path and tell you a story that touches you, so many people who have a past that affects you, so many partners that come into your life and teach you something. I am grateful and thankful to everyone who has directly or indirectly been associated with this book in the form of friends, acquaintances, designers, guides, beta readers, etc.

My heart is full of gratitude for a few friends who have shared their relationship secrets and trusted me in keeping their secrets a secret. Without their stories, this book would have been incomplete.

I would especially like to thank my author friend Diksha Pal Narayan for her guidance and valuable tips right from the beginning, and for also being my first beta reader.

Some friends have unknowingly helped me ease my anxiety by lending their ear whenever needed. In moments of despair, their light talks eased my tension and restlessness. Cheers to all of them!

Thanks, Mehedi, for the beautiful cover page and for

bearing with me. Sue, without you, I wouldn't have been confident of publishing this book. Thank you for editing it and giving me the valuable suggestions.

Lastly, I would like to thank my husband who has waited patiently for me to finish my book and has been supportive in my journey. His review, advice and stamp of approval mean a lot. Thanks for that!

God bless you all!